MURDER AT THE MANOR

A Northwest Cozy Mystery - Book 12

BY

DIANNE HARMAN

Published by: Dianne Harman
www.dianneharman.com

Interior, cover design and website by
Vivek Rajan

ISBN: 9781654692650

CONTENTS

ACKNOWLEDGMENTS

Years ago, when my husband and I were vacationing in England, we took a day trip into the countryside and ended up in a small village similar to Little Dockery. We ate lunch in a local pub and got to talking to some of the people who called the village their home.

They told us that our trip would not be complete without seeing the old English manor outside of town. They said it was very reminiscent of many old manors which had just become too expensive for families to take care of, and had ultimately been placed in the National Trust or English heritage in order to preserve their grounds and buildings.

The manor we saw must have been something in its day, but when we saw it, it was terribly rundown as were the extensive grounds it was on. I've thought of that manor often over the years, and when I decided to write a cozy mystery which takes place in an English manor, naturally it was my first thought. I have no idea what became of that manor, but I hope it's had as positive of an outcome as the one in Murder at the Manor.

Many thanks to the people in the pub who took their time to tell me about the manor and thanks to all of you for reading it!

And a huge thanks to all of the people who made this book possible.

And to Tom, for always being by my side, thanks!

Win FREE Paperbacks every week!

Go to www.dianneharman.com/freepaperback.html and get your FREE copies of Dianne's books and favorite recipes immediately by signing up for her newsletter.

Once you've signed up for her newsletter you're eligible to win three paperbacks. One lucky winner is picked every week. Hurry before the offer ends!

PROLOGUE

Cecil Boatwright-Jones had exhausted himself with all his yelling. He was the epitome of a crotchety old man. Well, he'd always been crotchety, even before he was old. In fact, the word crotchety may very well be too cutesy of a definition for what he was. He was so unpleasant that his own son, Richard, had absolutely nothing to do with him, not even a Christmas card, and it had been that way for over thirty years.

Richard held a very high-ranking finance position in London and frequently jetted out to Dubai and Saudi Arabia, never even giving his ailing father a second thought. He'd kept up the illusion of civility while Marie, Richard's mother and Cecil's wife, had been alive. But once she'd died after a short illness just before her sixtieth birthday, Cecil never saw hide nor hair of Richard.

It was one of his favorite topics to rant about.

And he had many.

Richard's disloyalty was right at the top of his list.

Then there was the ridiculous price of heating their drafty old mansion that had increased over tenfold in the past few years. As a consequence, their huge home was bitterly cold during the long British winters.

When it came to food, whatever he was served for dinner, even if he'd said he'd liked it the previous day, he'd complain that it was tasteless and improperly cooked.

And don't get him started on what was on TV. He insisted there was nothing interesting on television.

In short, he complained about anything and everything.

It was very difficult to be around him for any length of time. Actually, the only two people he saw with any regularity were his daughter, Cordelia, and his caregiver, Pat.

His grandson, Ptolemy, known as Toll or sometimes Tolly, came and went now and then. Tolly had turned out to be just as rude as his grandfather and had every bit as much venom in him as Cecil did.

But Cordelia and Pat were much gentler.

In Cecil's mind, Cordelia was a perfect example of what a woman should be. Quiet, subservient, polite, and beaten down. She conformed to his every whim. He enjoyed it when she'd plead with him to use some of his vast fortune to fix up the mansion. The roof was leaking in numerous places, rats scurried behind the wood paneling, and various bugs were eating into it. He enjoyed saying no, absolutely not.

His reason? Contractors couldn't be trusted. The antique specialists and historic building experts Cordelia found and brought to him were all 'charlatans' who charged far too much money and just wanted to take advantage of naïve old mansion owners, he'd told his daughter.

So, nothing got done.

Every time Cordelia came to see him, she looked more haggard and beaten down. Her long auburn hair had lost its shine decades ago, and now it was just a long frizzy mess. She had bags under her eyes and a permanent look of defeat on her face. He found pleasure in insulting her. It was a form of fun for him.

Pat was another matter. She was a professional caregiver and used to so-called 'crotchety' patients of which he was a prime example. She just ignored him and spoke to him in a kind of sing-song, almost 'baby' voice.

"Here you go, Mr. Boatwright-Jones, I've brought you a lovely bowl of porridge."

"Don't patronize me!" he'd growl, and turn the bowl over. He watched her carefully, because he really wanted her to snap.

But she never did. She'd simply laugh and say, "Who's a grumpy old thing today?" and clean up the mess.

She was extremely frustrating for him. She never reacted, no matter what he did.

"Oh, those are very naughty words, Mr. Boatwright-Jones," she'd say with a giggle, if he started to verbally abuse her. "I'll have to put you on a time out."

Many times Cecil had told Cordelia to fire Pat and take over his care herself. But that was the only time Cordelia didn't bow to him. She had more than she could do just caring for the house and garden and there was absolutely no way she could care for him full-time as well. Many were the nights she had to hurry to his bedroom when he cried out, because Pat had gone home to her own family.

He couldn't walk anymore and demanded constant attention.

If he could have walked, he would have slapped Cordelia around for not obeying his command to fire Pat. But he couldn't, so all he could do was yell at her, and although it was satisfying to see Cordelia look so distressed, she still wouldn't fire Pat.

So he was stuck with Perfect Pat. Perfect, indomitable Pat.

But he complained about her any chance he got, especially if she was in earshot. To Toll, to Cordelia, to dead Marie, to the wall, if necessary.

All in all, he was an extremely unpleasant man, and a complete burden for anyone who knew him.

Cecil didn't even pay Pat for her caring work. She did it as a charitable act.

He didn't like to pay anyone. He kept his savings tightly locked up and complained when Toll would let him know when an expenditure was necessary. Even buying something like teabags could spark one of his rages.

It was hardly a surprise when one night, after a particularly bad day, when he was sound asleep, worn out by all his complaining, someone snuck into his room in the dead of night.

They looked at his face with disgust. He had his mouth open, dribble coming out of it as he snored. The intruder, filled with absolute hatred and a sense of finally getting what they wanted, pulled a syringe out of their pocket.

They inserted it into Cecil Boatwright-Jones' neck and pushed the plunger down. They knew the injection would kill him within fifteen minutes, and they took great satisfaction in doing it.

A few moments later they snuck out of the room, looking back and smiling at their handiwork.

CHAPTER ONE

"Wow!" DeeDee said. "This is so cute!"

She was driving their rental car through the tiny English village they'd just arrived in, while Jake sat in the passenger seat. They'd shared the drive from Gatwick airport, changing places at a gas station along the way. Having a right-hand drive vehicle and driving on the left-hand side of the street was difficult to get used to, especially when they navigated through narrow country lanes.

"It is, isn't it?" Jake said with a grin.

And indeed, the village known as Little Dockery, and appropriately named for its size, was like a picture postcard.

All of the buildings in the village were constructed from yellow brick, and seemed a little higgledy-piggledy. Nothing was in a straight line. It was as if the buildings had simply made themselves comfortable over the hundreds of years they'd been there, and snuggled into the countryside together.

The village consisted of a few roads and a handful of cottages with little else. There was a post office next to a tiny convenience store, a very small church that was more of a chapel than a church, a village green with a bench and a duck pond, and a pub with an outdoor seating area. DeeDee had to stop the car when the ducks decided to waddle across the road in a line.

"Quaint is the word I'd use," Jake said, and they both laughed.

"This is such a change of scenery from what we see around Seattle," DeeDee said. "We may as well be in another universe."

They'd driven past acres and acres of farmland on their way, and no one would even suspect a village was located nearby. It was very quiet. They had the car windows down, and all they could hear was the chirping of birds and the rustle of the breeze blowing through the leaves overhead.

Everywhere they looked it was green with hedges and trees framing the yellow brick buildings. It was very charming and unlike anything they'd ever seen in the United States.

"Now I'm really curious what Dockery Manor will be like," Jake said. That was where they were headed. Cordelia had sent them directions to it, but there hadn't been any pictures.

"Yes," DeeDee said. "Me, too. When we looked it up on the internet, the photos were in black and white, so they must have been taken a long time ago."

"I hope they haven't modernized it too much," Jake said. "I love all the old history. When Cordelia got in touch with me, I went house hunting on an English website, looking for old mansions. They have many that are very traditional on the outside, but have been completely renovated on the inside, including all the modern conveniences. It kind of bothered me, because it doesn't seem right."

"I agree," DeeDee said. "When you've got history like that, you should preserve it. I hope Dockery Manor will be old-fashioned. Maybe even something like Downton Abbey. Now, stop talking, because you're distracting me."

They'd come to the end of the village and were back on winding country lanes that were only wide enough for one vehicle. "Am I going in the right direction?"

Although there was a GPS built into the car, they'd lost the signal that made it work, and it was stuck on a road they'd passed about fifteen minutes earlier. As a result, they'd had to resort to the map provided in the rental vehicle.

Jake looked down at it. "I think so. As far as I can see, you make a left, then a right, and then you should arrive at the gate. It looks like there's a long drive from the gate to get to the house."

"All right, let's see if we can find the place."

DeeDee followed Jake's instructions, but it seemed like they were going entirely in the wrong direction. They were surrounded by woodlands and fields, and it didn't look like there could possibly be any buildings in the area.

But suddenly, quite out of nowhere, a magnificent old gate appeared in front of them. It was badly rusted and had clearly seen better days.

"Aha!" DeeDee said, pulling the car to a stop.

"Let me get out and try the gate," Jake said. "Doesn't look like there's an intercom or anything."

DeeDee watched as Jake approached the gate and tried to open it. He pushed it a few times, the metal clanging, and finally got it to work. It squeaked noisily as he opened it, then he motioned for DeeDee to drive in.

When she got past the gate, she still couldn't see the house. There was only a gravel driveway mixed with mud and growing weeds which curved around a corner lined by equally unkempt hedges. She looked around while Jake closed the gate and got back in the car.

"It hasn't exactly been manicured, has it?" Jake asked.

"No," DeeDee said in agreement. "Though it might be a shame if it was. It's not completely wild though, more like somewhere in between." She drove slowly along the gravel-mud road.

"Yes, it looks like once it had been very grand and tended to, but no one has the time for it anymore."

"I'm not surprised," DeeDee said. "Look how big the place is." They still couldn't see the house, as she gestured to the left and the right. "You'd have to have a whole team of gardeners to take care of it."

They approached a turning spot with a large fountain in the middle of it. It had the same air as the gardens, like it had once been absolutely magnificent. The fountain was very tall with a statue of three women pouring water out of vases. It looked like originally water would have flowed out of the vases into the deep bowl of the fountain, but now it was all dried up. Moss and algae in various shades of green, yellow, and brown climbed up the ladies' legs.

They drove through the turning spot, past the fountain, and soon the mansion came into view. It was on their left and still quite far away.

"Oh my," DeeDee said, breathless.

"That's really something," Jake said.

It was enormous. In the front it had at least eight windows along each of the two stories, and there were more windows below the roofline, indicating a third floor. It looked like it had once been somewhat the same color as the cottages in the village, but now it was so faded and run-down it was impossible to envision what it had once been like.

The closer DeeDee got to the mansion, the more the feeling of being unnerved intensified.

What looked nice from afar, looked far from nice, as they

approached the mansion.

"Does the phrase haunted house come to mind for you?" Jake asked quietly."

"Yes, and then some," DeeDee replied.

Many of the windows were boarded up, especially on one side of the building which looked like it wasn't used, but there were other boards that had been attached to the mansion as well. The roof was sagging dangerously in the middle, like a giant had taken a massive scoop out of the top. Some of the spires around the doorways and windows were crumbling, and now resembled faceless creatures with weather-devoured wings.

Windows wept with black water stains. Someone had planted a little bed of flowers to the left of the huge entryway, presumably to brighten up the place, but in reality, by contrast, their vivid freshness just made the mansion look worse.

DeeDee assumed that the driveway had once been smooth cobblestone, but now, many of the cobbles had come loose, and the car bumped over them. On one side of the driveway rebellious weeds had pushed through and swayed in the light wind. Someone had pulled up the weeds on the other half of the driveway, and little clumps of mud were scattered everywhere.

The only vehicle in the driveway was a dilapidated old car with faded red paint, which looked like it might collapse at any moment.

"Good grief, what have we done?" DeeDee whispered to Jake. The car windows were still open, and she didn't want anyone to overhear her. "This reminds me of something I took my kids to at Disneyland when they were little. And if it's like this on the outside, I can't imagine what the inside is going to be like."

"I've been thinking the same thing," Jake said. "Well, if it's too bad, we can always get a hotel."

"I guess," DeeDee said. "Although it will probably be miles away from here." She giggled, making the best of the situation. "Or maybe we should pitch a tent in one of the fields."

As Jake looked up at the house, his brow furrowed. "Right now that's looking preferable to the mansion."

They got out of the car, and as they did, a woman came out of the front door of the house. She looked every bit as much of an old relic as the house did. She had exceptionally long and frizzy auburn hair, which was streaked through with gray.

She wore a long green tunic and old gray walking boots that had obviously seen better days. It was hard to tell, but it looked like they may have originally been black.

DeeDee's first thought was that the woman looked like a witch, and then silently scolded herself for even having that thought. The woman was smiling kindly at them, even with a little shyness, as she approached them.

"Hello, there," she said. Her voice was exceptionally cultured, like the Queen's English. "I'm Cordelia, and you must be DeeDee and Jake. I hope you had a pleasant journey." She shook their hands.

"Yes, it was fine, thanks," Jake said. "Nice to meet you, Cordelia."

"The pleasure is all mine, dear," she said. "You will come in and have some tea, won't you? Some biscuits and things, or, I suppose you call them cookies. And scones. I wanted to put on a full English afternoon tea for you. We used to do that a few afternoons a week when Mummy was alive, but I'm afraid we've let it fall out of tradition. Please, let me help you with your bags."

DeeDee opened the trunk. "Afternoon tea sounds lovely. I'm sure we can manage the bags. Don't trouble yourself."

"No trouble at all," Cordelia said briskly, taking one of the suitcases out of trunk. "I may be getting on a bit, but the old girl's still a workhorse. I do most everything around here, except for the help I get from John. You'll meet him soon. He's doing some weeding in the herb garden for me. Right, let's get going."

She barely stopped for breath when she spoke, though she seemed slightly embarrassed, and never really looked directly at them. She had beautiful green eyes, and DeeDee imagined that in her day she must have been quite a beauty. She wondered if she'd always been shy, with darting eyes, and a slightly hunched-over posture, or if that had come about in her later years.

Cordelia took off and they followed her to the grand front door, their suitcases bumping violently over the old broken cobblestones.

As Cordelia disappeared inside, DeeDee and Jake gave each other a look, as if to say, "Here goes nothing!"

CHAPTER TWO

Jake got his wish. The inside of Dockery Manor was historical, all right.

In fact, far too historical. All of the antiques and the ancient fireplace with its huge overhanging mantle, were covered in dust. There was dust everywhere. DeeDee had read somewhere that dust was mostly made up of dead skin cells. It wasn't pleasant wondering how many dead skin cells there were around them, and how long they'd been there.

But even more than the dust, the smell was the most overwhelming thing a person noticed when they first set foot inside Dockery Manor. The dry, decaying smell of things that were terribly old, permeated every room in the manor.

There was a huge grand staircase at the back of the hallway, going straight up, then ending in a little landing and splitting off into two more staircases, one to the left, and one to the right. On the wall behind the landing was a large stained-glass window depicting some sort of epic battle scene. Half of it was absolutely beautiful and gleaming clean, letting in beams of colored light, red, yellow, green, and blue, which came streaming in with the sunlight.

The other half hadn't been cleaned yet, and the colors gave off nothing more than a depressing, murky glow. It seemed that everything was so big, the driveway, the stained-glass window, to name just a few, that nothing could be cleaned all at once.

"I have to apologize for the state of everything," Cordelia said, setting the suitcase she'd brought in on the bottom stair. She laughed without a smile, obviously embarrassed. "The place is extremely hard to manage, and until the inheritance kicks in, I'm afraid it's just me and John, our sort-of handyman. Pat used to clean Daddy's room, but she doesn't like to come here anymore."

She sighed deeply. "And I can't say that I blame her." Then she put on a fake smile. "Anyway, at least the kitchen is clean. I make that a priority. And you needn't worry. Your bedroom and bathroom are sparkling clean with fresh linens and towels. Please, just put your suitcases here and come with me."

DeeDee and Jake left their suitcases by the one Cordelia had put down on the stairs, and followed her through a side door into a long hallway lined with huge old portrait paintings.

"My ancestors," Cordelia said, looking proud and happy for the first time since they'd arrived. "They're the reason I desperately want to revive and restore this place. I'm sure they're turning over in their graves at the state of it. Even the grounds are so overgrown you can't see the old Roman bridge."

There really wasn't anything polite DeeDee or Jake could think of to say in response, so they both kept quiet.

Cordelia led them into a cavernous kitchen, with a high ceiling and huge old-fashioned tables in the center of the room that served as kitchen islands. Pots and pans were hung up everywhere and bunches of herbs were strung up all over the room, drying out. It smelled wonderful, and it all looked and felt very clean.

DeeDee broke into a smile. "Now this is what I call a kitchen," she said. "I have my own catering business back in Seattle called Deelish. I'd kill to have a kitchen like this!"

Cordelia smiled a genuine, slightly shy smile. "Thank you. Obviously, I do like my herbs."

"If you wouldn't mind, I'd like to take a picture of it and send it to Susie, my business partner." DeeDee said.

"No, no, not at all," Cordelia said. "Please, go ahead."

DeeDee snapped a picture, which was totally Pinterest-worthy, and sent it to Susie on her phone.

Cordelia turned on an electric kettle, which looked rather out of place in the antique kitchen, then went over to the kitchen table and began placing little sandwich slices and dainty cakes and cookies on several three-tiered cake stands. She'd already laid out a gorgeous gold-rimmed tea set, which was as quaint and pretty as the village itself.

"Please, do sit down and make yourselves at home," she said. "I wonder how long you will be calling Dockery Manor home. Not for too long, I hope…" She caught herself. "I mean to say, you're very welcome. I only mean that I hope your investigation is successful and…. Well, you know."

"Don't worry, Cordelia," Jake said, taking his seat at the table. "We'll investigate your case as quickly as possible, so your name will be in the clear."

Unless she did it, DeeDee found herself thinking, uncharitably. But she couldn't help it. In all their experience investigating various cases, sometimes it really was the least likely suspect who was the culprit. But, DeeDee reminded herself, if Cordelia had actually killed her father, she wasn't about to hire Jake's private investigating firm to go poking around, was she?

Cordelia had learned about Jake and ultimately hired him to investigate the murder of her father, because she was an opera fan. She kept up with all the opera news around the world, and when Angel Bridges had been murdered in Seattle it had sent ripples throughout not just the opera world, but the mainstream world as well, since Angel Bridges was a famous movie star and opera diva.

DeeDee had been instrumental in solving the murder and bringing the killer to justice, but she'd also given credit to Jake's investigating firm, and the news of their success in solving the Angel Bridges murder case had spread like wildfire. They'd gotten so many inquiries that they simply couldn't take on all the cases, and they'd had to refer them to other detective agencies.

It had been very beneficial for them, because it meant they could stop working on the numerous suspected infidelity cases that had been the bread and butter of their private investigation business. Those cases involved spouses wanting a PI to trail their husband or wife to find out if they were cheating on them. In truth, Jake, and Al, Jake's partner in the investigating firm, found those cases to be extremely boring, so they were glad to have more exciting cases to sink their teeth into. DeeDee was glad, too.

The only person who wasn't that happy about it was Cassie, Al's wife and DeeDee's best friend. She was a restaurant critic and wanted Al to stay away from danger. Al was a former Mafia member (now totally reformed), and that fact alone made her nervous.

She'd made it very plain she wished Al would just get a boring job and stay away from the excitement and danger private investigators like Jake and him inevitably got themselves into. But the firm was doing so well, Al couldn't bring himself to leave, plus he loved the excitement of it all.

DeeDee was torn over it. She loved investigating with Jake and Al, even if her official job was the catering business. She loved the thrill of it. She loved helping innocent people seek justice, like they would hopefully do for Cordelia. She loved that it took away the monotony and boredom that was such a part of day-to-day life. She reasoned that her kids were grown and had their own lives, so what harm could it do?

But at the same time, she understood Cassie's feelings. Cassie, out of her love for Al, wanted to keep him as far away from danger as possible. Plus, her first husband had been murdered, and she didn't want to go through anything like that again.

Understanding both sides of the argument, it was hard for DeeDee. She considered both Cassie and Al to be very good friends. She only hoped it wouldn't take too much of a toll on their marriage, and that things would work themselves out over time.

For now, at least, Al was in Seattle, doing some due diligence for a French businessman who was planning to invest with a real estate developer there and wanted to make sure everything checked out all right. That was one of their low-risk types of cases, and Cassie felt very comfortable with Al handling it.

After they were seated at the kitchen table, Cordelia poured some boiling water into a beautiful teapot and brought it over to the table on an equally beautiful tray. "Here we are," she said. "I hope you two enjoy it. Please, help yourself to the sandwiches, cakes, cookies, and everything."

"This is a real treat," DeeDee said, looking at the sandwiches. There were smoked salmon and cream cheese, cucumber, and egg mayonnaise sandwiches. There were also a number of tiny little cakes, very small éclairs, and little tartlets with white icing and cherries on top.

"Have you had scones before?" Cordelia asked, gesturing toward some little biscuit-looking creations.

"I have," DeeDee said. "But only because I had a British friend who made them for me once. Have you, Jake?"

"No, I haven't," he said.

"You're in for a treat," Cordelia said. "You eat them with clotted cream and jam." She gestured towards two ramekins, one containing thick white cream, and the other with homemade jam. "The classic debate in England is whether the cream or the jam should go on the scone first."

DeeDee grinned at her. "And which one do you think should go on first, Cordelia?"

Cordelia's face brightened for a moment. "Jam, without a shadow of a doubt. Though I don't wish to influence your decision on this very important matter."

They all chuckled, but the merriment lasted only a moment, as Cordelia's brow furrowed with signs of worry. Both DeeDee and Jake noticed the change in her.

Jake reached inside his jacket and pulled out a small notepad and pen. "I hope you don't mind if we get started on our investigation right away," he said. "I think time is of the essence."

"I agree," Cordelia said. "As far as I'm concerned, the sooner you start, the better."

"All right," Jake said. "The first thing we need to know is who knew your father that would have had access to him at night. I presume you lock the gate and the front door at night?"

"The gate is never locked," Cordelia said. "I don't see much point in doing it. If anyone wanted to get in, they could simply climb over it, or climb over the wall, so we just leave it as it is. I do lock all the doors at night, but the way this place is, if someone wanted to get in, I'm sure they could. I try to walk through the whole house at least once a week, but... some areas are so..." She drifted off, looking deeply depressed.

"Okay," Jake said. "Somebody may have snuck in. But first, let's look at people who have a key or who were in the house on a regular basis."

"Yes," Cordelia said. "Well, of course there's me. Then there's John, the handyman."

"Okay," Jake said encouragingly. "Who else?"

"My nephew, Toll. His real name is Ptolemy, but nobody calls him that. Ptolemy Boatwright-Jones. It's rather an intimidating name, isn't it?" she said with a laugh. "Then there was Daddy's caregiver, Pat Ives, who lives in the village. Those are the only people who come here regularly. Oh, and Walter Smythe. He went to school with Daddy, and they were in business together. I'd say he came to see Daddy about twice a month."

"You're doing great," Jake said. "Anybody else you can think of?"

"No, not at all. So..." Cordelia began, but she didn't get to finish, as there was a knock at the front door. It sounded incredibly ominous, the huge door knocker clanging against the thick wood, like it was the Grim Reaper himself at the door. Cordelia looked even more concerned, if possible. "I'm coming," she said.

A moment or two later, she called, "Jake!" rather weakly.

Jake and DeeDee shared a worried look, then rushed out of the kitchen, through the hallway adorned with portraits of the ancestors, and into the vast entry, to find out what was going on. There were two very stern police officers at the door, staring Cordelia down.

"Who are these people?" the tall policeman asked, looking DeeDee and Jake up and down with barely veiled contempt.

CHAPTER FOUR

John Bowen had, to put it mildly, led an unconventional life.

It all started in Bristol, where he grew up in a small suburb with a bus driver father and a secretary mother. They had a decent life, and he and his brother, Paul, never wanted for anything. Well, that wasn't entirely true. They had toys and books and shoes and hot meals, and went out to play in the fields all hours of the day, and bathed in the nearby river in the summer. It looked like an ideal life. But John craved something more – excitement.

He felt like he never fit in, like he was destined for something greater. While Paul planned to, and eventually did become a bus driver like his father, living the same sort of life, in the same sort of Bristol suburb (though farther out, since prices had rocketed and the central location was no longer affordable), John had dreamed of being an intrepid explorer.

He filled his head with outlandish tales from novels and old accounts of explorers of the British Empire and was consumed by the romance of being an explorer-cum-pirate, a noble rogue, a likeable outlaw, who would break all the rules but succeed in the end and win acclaim and applause from everybody.

The problem was how to do this in the modern world.

He drifted out of school and toward a visionary, artistic crowd, who dabbled in psychedelics and dreamed of a new world where they'd build their own society and stick it to "the man." They lived in a squat, historic building they'd found empty and "captured" it. They lived there with their grand dreams, a great deal of intoxicating substances, abstract art, and without running water or electricity.

They were living the dream for a while, until one of them died of an overdose, and the group fizzled out. After that, a normal, boring life looked much more attractive to most of them, and they went back to the university and strived for jobs, cars, marriage, and 1.7 kids.

But John was hungrier than ever for something different. He joined a community of Hari Krishnas who lived on a farm in the Somerset countryside, and dabbled in Buddhism, Shamanism, and just about every other spiritual doctrine he could get his hands on.

He became a sculptor and woodworker, and was actually quite good at both. He'd make a coffee table or a bedside table if he really needed some money, but otherwise he tried to stay outside of society and their ideas of money and consumerism as much as possible.

Once he even had a contract carving magic wands to sell in a shop in Glastonbury, which seemed to be the English mecca for hippies, New Agers, witches, wizards, and other generally off-beat people. But that felt too commercial, so he stopped it.

He did end up living in Glastonbury for a while, though, in a tent in the forest. The place was said to be the legendary Isle of Avon, and King Arthur was supposed to be buried in Glastonbury Abbey.

He continued in this way, never aspiring to settle down or to own anything. He lived in communes, tents, broken-down old trailers, and spare rooms in the houses of artists or witches or whomever else was interesting to him.

Now, he was approaching sixty, living in Little Dockery in a run-down old shed he rented from a farmer for £30 a month, and having a full-blown midlife crisis.

What had he achieved during his lifetime? Nothing. Absolutely nothing.

He'd always been okay with that. John had always thought achievement was vain. It was just to show off. It was empty, vacuous, pointless, and devoid of meaning.

Who did he have to lean on? Paul didn't want to have anything to do with him. His parents were still alive okay, but they held entirely different values than he did. Although they were always kind to him, he knew they thought he was a failure.

Was he a failure?

He wasn't sure.

As he'd gotten older, it was harder to find anyone on his wavelength. The young people these days seemed to be more interested in getting a nice house and going on exotic vacations rather than sticking it to the system, and on the rare occasion when he did find a group of young rebels, he felt like an old relic.

People like him at his age were few and far between.

And the fact was, that even though he'd tried to deny it for the past ten years or so, he really was ready to settle down, but he didn't have the means to do it. He had no money to his name.

Thankfully, he also had no debts, because he didn't believe in them. The little ten-pound notes he got here and there from Cordelia was all he had to his name. Once he'd paid his rent and bought bread and instant noodles from the market, there was little left over. Sometimes he had to go without heating. He didn't have an oven or a refrigerator, just a microwave and an electric kettle.

Most of the time he spent his evenings sitting in front of a fire outside, eating dry bread or plain noodles, trying to find the inspiration that had once captured him in his youth. Back then, living the life he now had would have seemed romantic, cutting edge, and adventurous.

As time went on, he just felt poorer and poorer, and emptier and emptier.

And working at the Boatwright-Jones house had only exacerbated this. To John, Cecil Boatwright-Jones represented everything that was wrong with humanity. He'd inherited his wealth, lived in a house that was built on proceeds from West Indian slavery all those years ago, gave none of his money away, and thought the spiritual world was a load of old claptrap.

In fact, Cecil Boatwright-Jones and John Bowen were as polar opposite from each other as it was possible to be.

John was keenly aware he was begging for scraps from Cecil Boatwright-Jones through Cordelia, and this insulted his pride. But what else could he do? He didn't want to move again. He wanted to put down roots. He wanted to feel like he was part of a community. He just couldn't face another move. His mental health was at a breaking point.

So, he endured. He endured when, every time he'd pass by the large French doors in Cecil's room, Cecil would verbally abuse him.

Sometimes it was direct. "Get off my land, you scum!"

But what was worse and far more cutting, was when he addressed Pat or Cordelia, or nobody at all, and said things like, "Oh look, the ogre's back again. Won't someone tell him he's not welcome here." Then he'd chuckle cruelly to himself.

John never replied, perhaps because Cecil Boatwright-Jones was only echoing the horrible voices in John's head, and John didn't have the strength for a rebuttal. Cecil was very good at that, finding out peoples' weaknesses, and honing in on them with scarily accurate precision.

When John returned home after weeding the herb garden at Dockery Manor, he found his farmer landlord, Killian, sitting on the front step, the door wide open, drinking a cup of tea. John hated it when he did that, which was at least once a week, but he felt he couldn't say anything because he was getting his lodgings for practically nothing.

Killian had an excited look in his eyes. "Oh, John, did you hear about Cecil Boatwright-Jones?"

"He's been dead a while now, Killian," John said wearily.

"Ooh, yer' haven't heard. Poisoned, he was. Whole village's talking about it."

"Well, never mind."

"Oh, I know he was a bad'un, but yer' gotta have some sympathy for the man, being murdered and all."

"Not really."

Killian looked at him out of the corner of his eye, while John pushed by him to make his own cup of tea. "You didn't kill him, did yer'?"

"No. Wish I did. Prison'd be better than this."

"Oh, yer' a miserable old git. So... who d'yer' think did it?"

"The old beggar probably did it himself, hoping to ruin someone's life in the process by having them accused," John said.

"Ha!" Killian said, tickled by the idea. "You could be right about that. A lot of folk would have had joy in offing him, I'm sure. He had no respect for nothin' nor nobody. He would'er slapped Mother Mary on the bottom if she'd been cursed enough to meet him." Killian laughed at his own joke.

John didn't. He barely laughed at anything these days. He just continued making his tea.

Killian, as usual, was happy carrying the conversation on by himself. "Well, yer' gotta look at who stands to benefit. 'Course, Cordelia does, but she wouldn't hurt a fly, by my reckoning. That Toll boy looks like a suspect to me. A thug, he is. I'n't he?" He twisted back to look at John.

John shrugged.

"Or," Killian said, his eyes shining with excitement, "coulder' been that son of his, Richard, the one that's never here anymore. Coulder' snuck in and done the old sod in, payin' him back for his cruelty once and fer all."

John sipped his tea. "It don't interest me," he said.

"Little Dockery got a killer on the loose and yer' not interested?" Killian said. "Hmm… I'm going to keep my eye on you, John."

"Do what you want," John said. "I'm going to go to bed now."

"It's but 5:30, John."

John didn't even bother to reply. He just went to the tiny bed opposite the kitchen and sprawled out on it, fully clothed, as he always did. Killian remained on the step for a while, rolling a cigarette and whistling through his teeth, which was tremendously annoying.

John knew Killian was desperate to chat, but he just couldn't face anyone. He just couldn't.

CHAPTER FIVE

If you'd ever met Ptolemy Boatwright-Jones, you'd never forget him. It was not only his name that stood out from the norm, but just about everything else, too.

For one thing, he was six feet five inches tall.

For another, he had long blond hair that swept past his shoulders, which he often wore in a messy topknot on his head.

For yet another, he had numerous tattoos. Actually, he probably had more inked skin than uninked. He had teardrops tattooed under his eyes, and on his arms, legs, and chest, dragons, gargoyles, mermaids, and angels fought for attention. He liked to wear vests and cut-off pants to show them off. He also wore flip flops to showcase the skeleton tattoos on his feet, marking where the bones would be underneath.

This might have been somewhat less shocking if it weren't for his accent. He looked like a thug, but he spoke like a prince. His accent was similar to the Queen of England's, with perfect pronunciation.

His tastes, in combination with his background, meant that he was not really at home anywhere, and didn't fit in with any specific group. For the most part, his school friends from Eton were shocked and horrified by the way be looked, his penchant for gangster rap, and the fact he didn't go on to university. But he was far too posh to mix with the people he looked like. He was from a different world entirely.

So he spent a lot of time alone, and had just two friends, entrepreneurial types like himself. One was Aziz, who grew up in a poor family in Nottingham, but now owned a real estate firm that was just getting off the ground, and the other was Liam, better known as Professor Red, a rap artist from a middle-class family in Wimbledon.

Ptolemy had trained in accountancy, just to get his father, Richard, off his back. He found doing freelance accounting made him quite decent money, so he took on jobs here and there. But his real passion was foreign exchange trading, commonly referred to as Forex, and he stayed up night after night in front of his computer, making trades, and trying to become a multimillionaire.

In fact, money was the major thing on Ptolemy's mind, night and day.

He was making a good deal of money with accounting, but that wasn't nearly enough for the lifestyle he wanted to have which included jet setting around the world, partying with supermodels on yachts, and driving the fastest cars money could buy. So anywhere he could make money, he'd tried it.

He'd even dabbled in drug dealing for a time, and had made a master plan to smuggle hard drugs into the UK from South America, but ultimately decided the narcotics world was littered with far too many dangerous people. He wanted to remain alive, so he could spend his money.

But that decision didn't mean he was averse to a little lawbreaking. He siphoned money out of various accounts he worked for here and there, careful never to leave a pattern, careful to switch clients often, and change addresses just as frequently, so it would be hard to track him down.

Sometimes he even took accounting jobs under a fake name, Tom Smith, if he planned to take a lot of money. Each time he did it, he told himself, "This will be the last time." But there was always another Gucci coat to buy, and always something just beyond his reach that a little extra cash would help out with. It had become a habit.

He felt it was very unfair that he didn't have a trust fund. Liam, who's family was nowhere near as rich as his, had been gifted £200,000 for a deposit on a house before he'd gotten famous, whereas Ptolemy was given next to nothing.

"I paid for your education," Richard had said. "What else do you want? My father didn't give anything else to me."

And no amount of needling or whining changed his father's mind, so that was that.

As for Ptolemy's mother, she'd never been very interested in him. She'd shipped him off to boarding school at the age of seven, and pretty much washed her hands of him. Ptolemy had stayed at Dockery Manor during the school holidays - left to run wild by Cordelia and making it his mission to avoid grandfather Cecil's insults - and his only real memories of his mother were when she took him to London every October for a week of extravagant living.

"Isn't it wonderful?" she'd say to him, her eyes shining. "I don't know any other little boys with such a fabulous opportunity."

Granted, she would take him around Hamleys, the most famous toy store in the world, for one afternoon. But the rest of the trip was spent with her going out to posh bars and gallery openings, and leaving him in the fancy hotel room alone late into the night, with nothing but the TV and room service for company. Of course, Richard wasn't there because he was always working, and for most of Ptolemy's childhood, had worked in Hong Kong and Singapore. Ptolemy had never visited him.

Ptolemy hadn't spoken to his mother since his graduation from

Eton, where she'd turned up for half an hour, just to 'show her face,' and then had immediately gone back to her selfish schedule. Ptolemy didn't even get to speak to her that day.

He'd just seen her clapping during the ceremony, looking glamorous as ever and, of course, standing next to a handsome bored-looking man. Her red lipsticked mouth was set in a wide smile, showing off her pearly teeth, and she looked totally smitten with the man. Ptolemy guessed that she'd left the ceremony at the man's request.

He had no idea what she was doing now. She was from a very wealthy family herself, and always seemed to spend money like water, but he couldn't bring himself to find out her number, call her, and ask for money. He imagined he'd say, "It's Ptolemy," and she'd reply, "It's who, sorry?"

He still had what felt like an open, raw wound in his heart, and he couldn't give her the opportunity to stab him in it again. So he just tried to forget about her as much as he could. He carried on with his arrogant persona, like nothing in the world could possibly rattle him.

Unfortunately, though, there was a wrench in the works.

It was his new girlfriend, Kelsey. She came from a dirt-poor family in Yorkshire, the first in her family to go to university and have an office job.

"Tolly, you have to talk about the past," she said to him when they were lying in bed in his fashionable loft apartment in the city of Gloucester. "Otherwise it comes back to haunt you. You know, when you get angry at me sometimes for going out too much, well, what you say is over the top. You're not getting angry at me, you're getting angry at your mother. You just don't know it."

"You're quite the psychologist, aren't you?" he asked, rolling over to face away from her and picking up his phone. He pulled up his Forex stats to see how his decisions had paid off overnight. He swore. "I lost five thousand pounds last night."

"Tolly," Kelsey said, shaking him. "You have to fix your rage problems. One day you could really end up hurting somebody, like me. All my friends are telling me to leave you, and I know if I told my parents about how you treat me, they'd be furious."

"Fine, whatever, listen to them and leave me," he mumbled. "Just like everyone else does."

"No," she soothed. "I wouldn't. I haven't so far, have I? Even though I really should have by now. But I see the good in you, Tolly. I see that you don't want to be angry and smash things up and punch holes in doors, but you do it because of all the pain inside you. Because of the past. You need to process it and get it out, before it destroys everything you have."

"I'm making good money," he said.

Irritation crept into Kelsey's voice. "So money is all there is to life, is that it?"

"In this world, you're nothing without money."

"Are you saying my family's nothing?"

"That's not what I said."

"No," Kelsey said angrily, getting up from the bed. "But it's what you meant. If you had even half a brain in your head, you'd know there are things much more important than money. Like family. Like integrity. Like love."

Ptolemy still looked down at his phone, tapping away, though he wasn't really doing anything. The conversation was riling him too much. "Love is something only children believe in."

"So now you're calling me a child?"

"If the shoe fits."

"Fine." She stood there, staring him down, breathing angrily. "I don't have time for this. I have to get ready for work."

"Go on then."

She disappeared into the bathroom, but then angrily reappeared seconds later, talking with her toothbrush in her mouth as she brushed. "You see, the problem with you, Ptolemy, is that you think you're just too cool, too above everything that makes people human. You act like a robot, like you don't care, and then from time to time you explode, because you've been holding everything inside and bottling it up."

"Whatever."

"Remember when you got arrested for smashing the bottle over the guy's head in the pub? He hadn't even really done anything, just made a stupid comment about your hair. I mean, what you did isn't normal."

Ptolemy scoffed. "Who wants to be normal?"

"I do! Well, I don't want to be normal in the sense of just like everyone else, but I don't want to be living some violent lifestyle for no reason. I mean, who ended up suffering because of what you did? He just got a couple of stitches. You had to go to court and pay a massive fine, and I had to worry about you going to prison. So it's us that suffered more. Why can't you just be calm and get on with your life?"

True to form, Ptolemy exploded. He threw his phone across the room and jumped up to his feet on the bed. He screamed at her. "Just shut up! One minute you're telling me I don't feel enough, or some other baloney, that I'm too calm, then you're telling me to calm down. I can't win with you! Just get out and leave me alone."

Kelsey shrugged. "You've probably broken your phone."

"Who gives a darn? I'll just buy another one." He jumped down off the bed and went to retrieve his phone. Sure enough, the screen was shattered. "Whatever."

"You see?" Kelsey said, victorious. "Who suffers from your temper? You."

"Shut up," he said. He went into the kitchen and poured enough water in the kettle to make one cup of coffee. Then he sighed deeply, and poured enough water in for two. Listening to the sound of Kelsey getting in the shower, he made up two cups of coffee. One for himself, black with three sugars, and one for Kelsey, just the way she liked it, with milk and two sugars.

He looked down at his broken phone, then tossed it on the floor. Kelsey was probably right. His temper had gotten way out of hand. His sense of revenge and malice was getting worse over time, not better, and he had all kinds of violent fantasies playing out in his head.

To satisfy his need for all the money in the world, he'd even thought about getting involved in some violent robberies, but he hadn't gone through with it because of her.

He did love her, but he didn't know what a relationship even looked like. During his childhood, his parents were very rarely together, and when they were, they barely spoke. Even then, he saw both of them so infrequently, that often the only time he'd see them together would be on Christmas day, which was often a frosty affair at some posh London hotel.

He'd never seen any kind of template of how a man and woman should be together, in love and happy and respectful and warm. And he had so much emotional baggage he was bringing to the table. He didn't know how to calm himself down, because nobody had ever shown him how. He was so full of rage and discomfort and pain that it seemed to spill out all over the place when he least expected it to, like lava flowing out of a volcano, burning everything in its path.

Kelsey included.

As he stirred the coffees, he felt trapped thinking about it all. How could he resolve this? How could he learn how to treat her well so they could be happy?

What was he to do?

CHAPTER SIX

Pat Ives stood in the hallway of her tiny, crooked cottage, chatting on the landline phone. She'd lived there so long, in the heart of Little Dockery, that she was as much a part of the village as the little terraced cottage she shared with her husband, Michael. Their two sons, Nathaniel and Freddie, had grown up there in the very same cottage, and were now living in Finchingfield with families of their own.

They were "her special boys," even though they were in their 20's, and she doted on them, as she did her male grandchildren. Her daughters-in-law and female grandchild? Not so much. Her daughters-in-law were always getting things wrong.

Becky, Nathaniel's wife, couldn't keep an immaculate home. She was too busy at her very important job, which always made Pat roll her eyes. She thought Becky should have given up her job as a surgeon to take care of her little boy Callum, and she didn't miss a single opportunity to ram this message home to Becky.

And why was Becky so standoffish? She never took any of Pat's parenting advice, even though she was very generous with her corrections and gave her lots of hints and tips.

Lila, Freddie's wife, was a stay-at-home mum, at least, but she didn't do anything right, either. For one thing, she was far too glamorous with a full face of makeup, high heels, and blow-dried soft dark hair. She also went to the gym for three hours a week. "I didn't have time for any of that when my boys were young," Pat always used to say. "I was far too busy taking care of them."

Lila and Freddie had two children, a little girl Poppy, who was far too boisterous for Pat to take a liking to her, and a little boy called Noah. He was "granny's little prince" and was full of life and energy, bounding around with his red cheeks and a loud voice. "He's so healthy and happy," Pat would always say with a big smile, before giving him extra candy out of her purse.

She never missed an opportunity to tell her friends about Callum, and especially Noah, and right now she was doing so on the phone to her church friend Diana. Pat was secretly pleased that Diana only had daughters, and only female grandchildren. "So," she asked, "do you think Sophie will get pregnant again? She really needs to give you a grandson!"

"Oh no," Diana said. "She's too busy with her beauty business. Things are really picking up, so she's going to need to employ a part-time nanny. She's doing so well, in fact, that she's going to employ a cleaning lady for a couple of days a week as well."

"A cleaning lady?" Pat asked. "I couldn't bear to have a stranger in my house. They might steal things."

"Oh, well, I'm sure she'll have cameras installed or something," Diana said. "But Pat, I must tell you something I found out."

Pat was all ears. She loved good gossip. "I'm listening."

"Reverend Gregory," the female out-of-town vicar who'd been appointed to their local church a few months ago after their long-serving, home-grown vicar Reverend Copley had passed away due to old age, "was seen getting out of a strange man's car down in one of the back lanes this morning. Then she walked into the village."

"So nobody would see her," Pat said. "My, my, I wonder what's going on there."

"That's what I was thinking," Diana said. "Do you think she's husband-hunting?"

"Could be," Pat said. "Did you get any information about what the man looked like? Who saw it happen?"

"It was Yvonne. She was walking her dogs in the field where Killian lets his horses graze, and was just coming up to the gate. The vicar didn't see her. She said he was a youngish man, perhaps in his early 40's, and driving a very nice shiny car. She didn't know what make it was, but she said she was sure it was very expensive."

"Reverend Gregory is 53," Pat said with authority. She made it her business to know these sorts of things. "So if it's a romantic interest, she's got a wealthy toy boy on her hands."

"I know!" Diana replied. "I'm sure it'll be quite a scandal if it gets out. Don't tell anybody, will you, Pat? I don't want to create any kind of trouble for her. Although some of the congregation was extremely hesitant at the idea of a female vicar, and I was on the fence myself, I think she's doing a very good job."

"Hmm," Pat said. "I won't repeat it, I can assure you."

"Will you come by for some cake later on?"

"I'll try," Pat said. "I'm rather busy today preparing for the flower arranging class tomorrow. I'll be going into town for the flowers tomorrow, of course, but I have to decide what the students will make, and sort out everything."

"Yes, of course," Diana said. "It's coffee cake. I'll be sure to save you a slice in case you can't pop over until tomorrow."

"Thank you, Diana. See you, then."

"Toodle-oo."

Immediately, almost before the receiver had hit the cradle, Pat dialed Yvonne's number.

"Yvonne!" Pat said. "Are you still coming to flower arranging tomorrow?"

"Hi Pat. Yes, I am. Why, is there a problem?"

"No, not at all," Pat said. She spun a white lie. "I'm just checking up on everybody to be sure of the numbers. I'm going to get some rather expensive flowers for us to work with, and I don't want to buy too many."

"Ah. Well, yes, I'll definitely be there."

"So... how are the dogs?"

"The dogs?" Yvonne sounded confused. "They're absolutely fine."

"I'm sure they're enjoying their walks."

"Yes...?"

"I do think it's good you get out for that exercise every day with them. I do some walking myself, as you know, but sometimes I have to admit I skip a day. I'm a human, not a robot! But, with dogs, they sort of make the decision for you, don't they?"

"Yes, I suppose they do."

"The only thing is, I suppose they might frighten other animals. How do Killian's horses respond to them?"

"Oh, Larry and Toby aren't at all aggressive. Golden Retrievers are big softies, Pat. They jump when a butterfly flies past," Yvonne said, chuckling.

"Ah, right. Sorry I don't know much about pets. I'm allergic to cats and dogs, so I'm afraid my experience is limited."

"Yes, I think I knew that."

"Hmm. I'm not allergic to horses, though, which is a good thing, because I often walk through the field where Killian's horses graze. You take that route, too, don't you?"

"Yes, I do quite often."

"Sometimes it gets muddy, though, which I dislike if I wear my nice walking shoes. Hmm, did you go there today, Yvonne? Is it muddy today? Should I wear my wellington boots?"

"I did," Yvonne said. "It wasn't too bad. I think walking shoes or sports shoes would be absolutely fine. No need for boots."

"Thank you, Yvonne. That's very helpful." She was silent for a moment, to give Yvonne a chance to come out with the gossip, but Yvonne stayed quiet. Pat rolled her eyes and switched the phone to her other ear. "So… do you think Reverend Gregory is doing a good job?"

"Yes, I do. I liked her as soon as I met her, and I'm glad to say my instincts haven't been proven wrong. I think she's a fine addition to the village. She brings a fresh perspective."

"Oh, yes, I quite agree," Pat said. She couldn't care less, really. She said whatever sounded good at the time. "I do think it's a shame for her, though."

"What? What's a shame?"

"Not having a nice man to share her time with. After all, she has quite a lot of time on her hands, with this being such a small village. I just think she might be lonely, and would be happier with a companion. Don't you think?"

"She seems quite happy to me," Yvonne said. "Not everybody has to have a partner."

"Oh yes, I know, the world has moved on," Pat said. "We have all different kinds of household set-ups these days. But a woman still has a woman's heart. And I don't know any woman that wouldn't like the company of a kind man. Hmm, I wonder. Have you seen her with anyone?"

"Well, now that you mention it…" Yvonne began.

A huge smile spread over Pat's face. She was a master at this sort of game. She got ready to milk every last detail of the situation from Yvonne. By the end of the conversation, Pat had found out that this man had short brown hair, with a touch of gray at the temples, drove what she deduced was probably a 3- or 5-series BMW in dark blue, had a professional job of some kind (he was wearing a suit at the time), and had smiled at Reverend Gregory in a way that "left little doubt that he was most fond of her," as Yvonne put it. They hadn't kissed, nor held hands.

"But that doesn't mean anything," Pat said. "She's bound to be very strict about any sort of physical contact because of her position in the church. Hmm, well, Yvonne, I don't think you should tell anyone else. We wouldn't want to spoil things for the vicar, would we? Especially when she's just winning the hearts of the naysayers who wanted a man in the role."

"Yes, you're probably right," Yvonne said. "Well, see you tomorrow at flower arranging."

"See you."

"Oh, one thing," Yvonne said. "You might want to know because of the church coffee. There are a couple of Americans staying at Dockery Manor."

"Really?" This was most interesting.

"Yes. A married couple. I didn't talk to them much, only to know they were American, and that's where they were staying, with Cordelia, of course. Perhaps you'd like to invite them along."

"What a good idea, Yvonne. Maybe I'll pop over there, although it brings back such dreadful memories of Cecil. Poor man. I've had some nightmares about what that horrid person did to him. I do hope they're caught soon."

"So do I," Yvonne said. "But…" she said, lowering her voice, even though it was absurd to do so on the phone, "I think it was that dreadful Tolly or Toleny or whatever ridiculous name he's called."

"Ptolemy," Pat said, delighted to be able to enlighten Yvonne. "With a silent P."

"A silent P? Whoever has heard of that?" Yvonne said. "Like I said, ridiculous. Anyway, it's clearly him. He's a thug, and I'm sure he did it hoping to inherit."

"It's very sad to think Cecil's own grandson could have murdered him," Pat said. "Very sad, indeed. What has the world come to these days? Is there no such thing as family loyalty? Young men prepared to commit atrocious evil, just to inherit a few thousand?"

"I'll agree it's an atrocious evil," Yvonne agreed. "I won't agree it's a few thousand. More like a few hundred thousand, if not more."

Pat laughed. "How the rich live, eh?"

"Just goes to show, though," Yvonne said, "money can't protect you. When it's your time to go, it's your time to go."

"That's true enough," Pat said. "Oh, Michael's calling me, I must dash." It was a total lie, as Michael was out in the garden doing the weeding, but she couldn't wait to get off the phone to go and discover what she could about the Americans. Also, she'd make a point to stop and talk to Reverend Gregory, to see if she could pick up any clues about her love life.

Goodness, what an exciting day.

CHAPTER SEVEN

DeeDee and Jake took a lovely early morning walk through the fields. Being late spring, it was quite warm, but they still had to wear light jackets.

"I miss Balto and Yukon," DeeDee said. "They would have loved this." She was talking about their adorable husky dogs. They really hadn't wanted to leave them behind, but Cassie and Al were very competent and willing dogsitters.

Jake laughed. "I'm sure they're loving the attention they're getting at Cassie's, what with all the treats she gives them. When we return, I expect they'll be double the size they were when we left them!"

DeeDee giggled. "True enough."

When they'd returned, Cordelia had met them outside and called them into the kitchen. She gave each of them a steaming cup of tea and fixed them a traditional English breakfast. "Ever had an English fry-up before?" she asked.

"Can't say that I have," DeeDee said with a smile. "What does it involve?"

"Usually blood pudding, but I can't abide that, so I don't make it. So we've got sausages, bacon, scrambled eggs, fried bread, fried tomatoes, fried mushrooms, and baked beans. It may be a heart attack on a plate, but I've had plenty in my time, and my heart's still ticking away just fine."

"Sounds awesome!" Jake said.

"And it must always be accompanied by hot, sweet tea," Cordelia said. "That's the law. Sometimes it's called a builder's breakfast. There used to be a greasy spoon in the village, but now you have to go to the next town over if you want a fry-up. I just prefer to do it at home. It's going to take a few minutes, so feel free to come back in ten minutes, or stay here. Whichever you'd prefer.

"I've heard that our fried bread is quite similar to what the Native Americans in the U.S. call fry bread. I always wondered if the English took their fried bread recipe there and it was converted into fry bread. Whatever. We think it's wonderful."

"I've had fry bread and it's one of my favorites. I'm looking forward to it, and I think I'll stay here. I'm enjoying it," DeeDee said. The door to the garden was open, bringing in a pleasant breeze, and the kitchen surroundings were rustic and cozy.

"Good," Cordelia said with a slight smile. "Please let me know if you want any more tea. Three cups for breakfast isn't unusual for me." She got the ingredients out of the refrigerator and freezer and got started on the enormous fry-up. "John may come by today, so I'll make him a portion, too, just in case."

"Ah, yes," Jake said. "Actually, we wanted to start interviewing people today, and we thought John would be a good place to start. So you think he'll be over here later?"

"Impossible to predict," Cordelia said. "Sometimes he's here, sometimes he's not. Unpredictable as the English weather, that John is."

DeeDee noticed she spoke about him rather fondly. She wondered if there was some kind of romance, or at least warm feelings, brewing between the two of them.

"I'm assuming he doesn't have a phone then?" Jake asked.

"You'd be right," Cordelia said. "Half the time, we don't either. The landline was cut off many years ago, and it's only sometimes my ruddy mobile phone decides it will deign to hold some charge for me. Otherwise it simply won't turn on."

"I see," Jake said. "Do you know where we can track John down? I think we need to be proactive, rather than waiting around for people to come to us."

"Well, he may be at the little place he rents from Farmer Killian," Cordelia said. "But that's only a maybe. I'm not sure where he goes or what he does. I do know that in a former life he used to live in the forest in a tent. Not around here, somewhere else. I really don't know where, but I know that he feels comfortable in those sorts of surroundings. I expect he spends a lot of time in the woods."

"I see," DeeDee said, getting the sense that John was somewhat unusual. "Which woods do you think we should go through?"

"I'd go see if he's at the house at Farmer Killian's first," she said. "I better draw you a little map to show you how to get there. It's within walking distance, if you go through the fields, or you could drive, although it's a little farther because you have to go around the houses. If he's not at his house, there are some woods nearby. Let me draw you a little diagram."

"I just remembered," DeeDee said. "We have a map in the car if that would help."

"That would be excellent," Cordelia said. "Then I can show you exactly where it is."

After the fry-up, with Cordelia's drawing, map in hand, and walking boots on their feet, they set off through the fields to find John.

"That fry-up was absolutely delicious. And the fried bread is almost identical to the fry bread my mom used to make, even down to the honey," DeeDee said. "But it's very heavy on the stomach. I feel like taking a nap, not walking through the fields."

"Really?" Jake said. "I love it. I could eat that every single day. That would be a great way to start the day. In fact, I might even start making it when we get home."

"You'll be the size of a house in a matter of weeks if you eat that every day!"

Jake laughed. "True enough. I'll have to take Balto and Yukon on more walks."

"If anything's going to get me, it's these afternoon teas. I love those scones, and I think they'll be really easy as to make at home."

"Will you be able to find clotted cream, though?" he asked in a posh British accent that was very convincing.

"Good question," DeeDee said. "I have no idea. I'm sure that whole English afternoon tea thing could be a good arm for the business, though. You know, for baby showers, bachelorette parties, and occasions like that."

"I agree, I think it would be very popular," Jake replied. "Especially with champagne, like Cordelia said they sometimes do."

"Hmm, yes. The whole aesthetic lends itself to a celebratory mood, so the champagne would go perfectly."

Jake stopped. "Huh? What did you just say? The whole aesthetic lends itself... I can't remember. I just know you've been spending far too much time around Cordelia. You're already starting to form sentences like a British aristocrat."

"Okay then, dahhling." She linked her arm in his and pulled him along. "Come on." She sighed. "I always thought it would be quite glamorous to be a lady of the manor type, but up close, it's so different, isn't it?"

"I imagine the main thing is money," Jake said. "Those big old houses are money pits. If you have a fortune to spend fixing everything, you'll be fine. If not, you're going to have a very stressful life."

"Yeah, you're right. Probably why not many people own these houses anymore. Cordelia said most of them are now owned by the National Trust or turned into hotels. That's why she's so adamant about keeping Dockery Manor. It would be one of the rare gems that's being kept in the family."

"We've got to work this out for her," Jake said. "To help her clear her name, get her inheritance in the bank, and start fixing everything up."

"Yes," DeeDee said, as she snapped into an investigating mode. "This John Bowen sounds like a real character. He'd been living in a tent in the forest, Cordelia said. I wonder why that was. Homelessness, or out of choice?"

"I think the former is more likely," Jake said, "but who knows? I guess we'll have to find out."

"Maybe he's a modern-day hermit type," DeeDee mused. She looked down at the map. "When we get to the gate, we turn left, go down the lane, and his house should be on the right."

They followed her directions, but when they got to the spot where the house was supposed to be, they looked at each other with furrowed brows.

"This can't be it," DeeDee said, looking at the tiny little ramshackle shed in front of them. "It can't be."

Grass was growing wildly all around it, and it didn't look fit for human habitation. DeeDee wouldn't have even put a dog in there, much less a person. So when the front door swung open, and a man stood in the doorway, she jumped, not quite believing what she was seeing. This was his home? She felt a physical pang of empathy in her chest for the man standing there. This shouldn't have been anyone's home.

"Hi there," she said cheerily, waving. He didn't look at all approachable, but she didn't let that put her off. *He was just... untamed,* she thought, charitably.

He raised his hand and looked at each of them warily, but he said nothing.

"I'm Jake, and this is my wife DeeDee. By any chance are you John Bowen?"

He eyed them with suspicion. Eventually he said, "Yes," but it seemed to take a lot of effort. DeeDee got the impression he didn't like to talk very much. Perhaps she'd been right about the hermit thing. For some reason, she immediately took a kind of protective liking to him. She got the impression he was fragile, despite looking like some kind of yeti with his scraggly beard and unruly mane of frizz-curl, that appeared to be matting in places.

He must have seen her looking at it, because he began to pull it back into a very rough braid.

"I hope we're not disturbing you," DeeDee said.

John shook his head. He gestured toward the front step. He spoke, but his voice got lost, so he had to clear his throat and try again. "That's all I've got, in the way of seats. Sorry about that."

"It's fine," Jake said.

He looked like he was going to stay standing, but DeeDee thought they should honor his efforts at hospitality. It might warm him to them. So she sat down, and gestured for Jake to as well. It was a little awkward, as the doorway was narrow and it meant John was behind them.

"Tea?" he said.

"Yes, please," DeeDee said.

Jake nodded. "That would be great, thanks."

John, unsurprisingly, didn't say anything while he made tea for DeeDee, Jake, and himself. For a moment, none of them spoke, and DeeDee took in the sounds and sights of nature. Actually, when you were inside the doorway and looking out, the surroundings were lovely – with a hedgerow right in front that had butterflies and birds fluttering around it, perching, then soaring off again.

On one side, the fields rolled gradually up a hill and there was a woodland on the other side of the road. It wasn't close to a street, and even if it had been, the streets were so quiet it wouldn't be much of an intrusion. The entire area was completely devoid of human noise or of cars whizzing past. It was another world altogether.

Maybe John spent so much time outside it didn't really matter to him where he lived, DeeDee mused.

"Here you are," John said, handing them their mugs from behind. They both thanked him. He stepped between them and outside. He sat down on the ground in front of them, obviously not fazed by the lack of chairs. It surprised DeeDee, but that simple action told her they were more welcome than she'd previously realized.

"We're staying at Dockery Manor," Jake said. "We know that Cecil Boatwright-Jones was murdered." He was telling John the bare details, not wanting to give too much away about what they knew, not even that Cecil was poisoned. "We were wondering if you know anything about it?"

John sighed. "People die all the time. He was an old man. Thousands like him died on the same day."

"He was murdered, John. That's what's different about his death," DeeDee said.

John shook his head, grimacing. "Killed himself. I'm sure of it." He sipped his tea and avoided eye contact.

"What makes you think that?" Jake asked.

John sighed deeply, as if conversation was extremely taxing for him. "So Cordelia would have a hard time getting his money, because people would think it's her? I don't know. It's none of my business."

DeeDee certainly hadn't thought of that possibility. "Why would he want to do that?"

"If he could give anyone a hard time, he'd do so. He was… warped. Yes, that's the word. Warped."

"Do you know why?" DeeDee asked.

"No, and I don't care why," John said. "Psychoanalyzing people is a useless distraction, I've found. I take people at face value now."

"So you're the handyman up at the manor?" Jake asked.

John snorted. "That's a fancy title. I do odd jobs here and there for Cordelia."

"Hmm," DeeDee said, nodding. "What did you hear about the murder? How did it all happen?"

"I was there that day," he said, "working in the herb garden. I do quite a lot in there. Cordelia likes it, so I suppose I try to keep her happy. Cecil had one of his usual ranting fits. I could hear it all the way out in the herb garden. He was shouting at Pat, then he shouted at Cordelia when she came to see what was going on.

"When she came back in the kitchen, I saw her wipe away a tear when she didn't know I was looking. I tried to cheer her up and have a bit of a chat with her. I went home about 5:00 p.m. Next morning, I came to trim some of the bushes out back. After a few hours, I went to the house for a cup of tea and Cordelia told me he's dead and for some reason police suspected foul play. Can't say I know why."

DeeDee made a mental note they'd have to find out why themselves. Maybe Cordelia would know. She certainly hoped so, as she didn't look forward to visiting the odious policeman.

"If he didn't kill himself," Jake said, "do you have any idea who could have done it?"

John grimaced and shook his head. "Wouldn't do no good for me to speculate."

"Do you have an alibi?" DeeDee asked. "In case the police come knocking on your door? Anyone who knew you were here?"

"Spoke to Killian when I got back, that's the farmer who rents me my place, but that's no good, is it? I could have snuck out in the night and got access through the back. I have the key to the back door. I could have done it, but I didn't, because I'm not a murdering psychopath."

He scattered the dregs of his tea on the grass next to him. "To be honest, I don't think I can help you anymore. Even if I did have any evidence or speculation, who's going to believe me? I'm a failure in the eyes of society. A non-person."

DeeDee was horrified. "Don't say that! You're a human being, just like anyone else and worthy of the same respect."

John smiled at her sadly, and his eyes showed her how lowly he regarded himself. "Yeah. Well…" He got up from where he sat and hovered awkwardly, making it plain he wanted them to leave.

They got up as well and Jake shook his hand. "Pleasure to meet you, John. Thanks for talking with us."

John gave his hand a quick shake, but quickly drew his own hand back and jammed it in his pocket. He nodded at them both, avoiding eye contact, then went back inside his shack.

CHAPTER EIGHT

Walter Smythe was in deep financial trouble, extremely deep financial trouble. It was like falling into a deep, dark pit, hurtling into the blackness, and not knowing where the bottom was, even if one survived the impact.

Every night he stared at the ceiling while he was lying in bed unable to sleep, his mind racing, wondering how on earth he was going to prevent himself from going bankrupt. He knew he was very close to it happening.

What a dreadful thing to happen in his 80's, when all his life he'd managed to maintain not one, not two, but three families, all in the lap of luxury.

Walter Smythe was no humanitarian, because all three of the families were his own families.

The first of his families was with his Belen, a once-gorgeous Spanish woman he'd met at a stock market conference in London in 1960. He worked as a stockbroker, and she was a secretary to a Spanish colleague of his. They'd had a raging affair, and she'd left her husband for him. They had three daughters, Maria, Emilia, and Paula, all educated at the finest school in England for girls, Cheltenham Ladies' College.

When the girls were fourteen, twelve, and ten, his own private stockbroking firm had taken off, and his working hours were drastically reduced. He'd decided he needed to take up a new hobby. Perhaps golf, he'd mused, or buying a plot of woodland to tend.

But in the end, he settled on having a mistress as a much more exciting pastime, and his wealth and tall, handsome good looks had helped him snag Simone, an aspiring French model living in London. She was young, naïve, and pliable, but also rather feisty, and they had passionate arguments which helped to add a spark and sizzle to his life.

His "little hobby" as he referred to her when speaking privately to friends and colleagues, over time, became something more serious. In fact, he fell in love with her, head over heels in love with her, far more than he'd ever been with Belen. He considered leaving Belen for Simone, but he knew he wouldn't be taken seriously in professional circles with the little wisp on his arm, so he kept them both.

Simone lived in a gorgeous London apartment at his expense, and he stayed with her Monday through Thursday, returning to Belen Friday through Sunday. Soon she was pregnant with their son Barnaby, and that made family number two.

He ticked along quite nicely with that two-family arrangement. Simone knew about Belen, but Belen didn't know about Simone, and life was comfortable and fun.

But then someone came in and added a whole new dimension to his life. And that someone was Miranda St. John. It seemed that with each new 'wife,' they became feistier and feistier, and Miranda was the feistiest of them all.

She was actually Lady Miranda St. John, from a very aristocratic family. She was an excellent horse rider (specializing in show jumping), a very good shot (she loved pheasant hunting), and an overall take-no-nonsense sort of woman. She always wore red lipstick, even if the rest of her outfit was decidedly less glamorous, traipsing around the countryside with a Barbour jacket, wellington boots, and a flash of red lips.

She quickly found out about both Belen and Simone through undertaking her own research when noting his absences, and told him that he absolutely and categorically must split with them both, pay them incredible amounts of child support and alimony, and come and live in a cottage with her in the countryside. She was a freelance publicist and could fax her work back to the office in London from anywhere.

He swiftly complied with all her demands. She was a woman in charge, and in control, and actually, the thought of her telling him exactly what to do was quite comforting. So he divorced Belen, giving her the house, gifted the posh apartment to Simone, and paid through the nose for extremely expensive schooling for his four children.

Miranda St. John, who didn't change her name to Smythe, and actually laughed at the idea she would, had said to him, "If you think I'm giving up my ancestral name, you've got another think coming, Walter." She brought his grand total of children to five. She was forty-four when she gave birth to their daughter, who she decided to name Phillippa (Walter did not get any sort of say in this), and after that said, "No more. I'm not going to be in the kitchen, barefooted and pregnant, while you're out making money. No siree."

She began to work as soon as she got back from the hospital, between Phillippa's feeds. She was a formidable woman. Unsurprisingly, Phillippa grew up to be rather formidable, too, and an extremely accomplished showjumper, who won awards from competitions all around the country.

All of this swirled around in Walter's head in a horrible chaos, the sucking whirlpool of his money situation becoming ever greater with each day.

He'd paid for lavish Christmases for each family. He'd paid for Phillippa's horse and Paula's fashion addiction. He'd paid for first class flights to the Seychelles and Australia for family holidays he hadn't attended. And, most of all, he'd paid huge sums of money to each child for their own London apartments when they'd graduated from university and had started working. If he had to count how much he'd spent over the years, he was sure it would run into the millions.

Now, there was nothing left. And he was incredibly in debt.

There was no one to talk to about it, either. The shame would be too great. Not even Cecil Boatwright-Jones, when he'd been alive, his greatest friend. In fact, especially not Cecil Boatwright-Jones. Cecil always laughed at Walter's expenditures, saying he would never dream of supporting his children in such a way.

They went to boarding school, yes, but other than that they had the absolute basics, and he certainly hadn't paid out any money for apartments or houses for Cordelia and Richard. "They have to make their own way in life," he always said. "It builds character." But the real reason he didn't pay was because he couldn't bear to part with a penny more than was absolutely necessary, even for his own children.

Walter and Cecil owned shares in a company together, a business consultancy that they both used to work in, but had now handed over to a CEO and a group of handpicked consultants. It was doing very well with prestigious clients falling over themselves to pay hundreds of thousands to work with them - from London to Hong Kong to Dubai. They'd also had great success in Nigeria.

Cecil Boatwright-Jones had left all his profits in the company in the last couple of years. He'd said, pompously, "What's the use of me drawing out a few thousand pounds here and there" - talking about a six-figure sum - "when I can just wait until it gets to a million and then take it out." At the time of his death, his balance was 960,000 pounds. He'd died a little too early to cash out and collect his million pounds.

On the other hand, Walter had taken money out as soon as he could to pay for his huge living expenditures and plug holes in an investment opportunity that had gone terribly wrong. He'd taken over a boutique London hotel, but it had failed miserably, and he was in serious debt to creditors. Sometimes he felt like running off to Panama or perhaps Cuba, changing his name, and forgetting about all of them, the creditors, Miranda, his children, his exes, all of it.

But he was quite sure Miranda would hire a private investigator and track him down, even if it took years. She was just that kind of a woman.

He turned over in bed and watched her sleeping. He wondered if he could confide in her. He had a little tug in his desperate heart, wishing he could. He was so lonely. But very quickly, he admonished himself. He didn't want to burden her with it. Besides, he could fix it himself. He could. He knew he could

Since he wasn't getting any sleep whatsoever, he got up and padded downstairs in his slippers. He switched the kettle on to make a cup of tea, and decided to call his accountant James Elstone, who was in the Caribbean on an extended vacation.

"Walter," James said far too happily, his voice slurring.

"Are you drunk?" Walter said, disgusted. He had nothing against drinking, and enjoyed getting intoxicated himself. He was just so self-centered that he thought because he was dealing with such a serious problem, everyone else should be serious, too.

"No, my dear friend, just living the good life!"

Walter sighed. "I'll talk to you tomorrow once you've nursed that hangover."

"Jolly good!"

Walter slammed down his phone on the kitchen table, absolutely incensed. Not surprisingly, it didn't take much to get him incensed these days.

He made his tea, drank it too quickly, and scalded his tongue, which made him even more furious.

Without thinking, he stormed out of the back door of the cottage and went into the garden. There was a large pond, and he wondered about throwing himself in. Could he manage to drown himself? Perhaps if he moved that large rock and placed it on his chest. But it would be a horrible way to go, he thought. And horrible for Miranda to find him in such a way, so he didn't. If he was going to kill himself, he thought pills would probably be the best option.

But how could he kill himself? It would be terribly bad for his image, his legacy.

He made up his mind. He'd have to find a way to get Cecil's money out of the business, and into his own bank account. That's what he'd called James for, but he hadn't been totally sure.

Now, he was absolutely certain.

There was no other way.

CHAPTER NINE

DeeDee and Jake, feeling like they'd gotten nowhere with John, trudged back through the fields to Dockery Manor.

"I think we should split up," DeeDee said.

"What?" Jake said, panicking.

DeeDee laughed. "Oh, not like that, silly! Not break up. I mean split up, so you investigate one thing, and I investigate another. I don't think it makes all that much sense us for us to go everywhere together. We've got a lot of people to see and things to investigate, and we'll get double the amount done if we each do our own thing."

"I think you're right," Jake said. "Just don't put yourself in any dangerous situations. I wish you had Balto and Yukon to go with you."

"I'll be fine," DeeDee said. "You shouldn't worry so much. I can take care of myself. Besides, if I need any help, I'll call the police, and I'm sure they'll help."

"We're in the middle of nowhere. I imagine it would take them a long time to come down these winding country lanes. Especially if someone's going the other way."

They'd had plenty of unfortunate experiences with that while they were driving to Little Dockery from the airport. In places, the road was only wide enough for one vehicle. If you met another one, you had to screech to a halt to avoid a head-on collision, and then one party had to reverse enough until there was a little passing space. Even then, it was tight, and the vehicles had to crawl past each other at a snail's pace to avoid an accident.

"I'm sure it'll be absolutely fine," DeeDee said decisively.

"I'm just having terrible visions of you being injected with poison when the killer knows you're onto them."

"Stop it!" DeeDee said. "Don't you think I worry about you, too? Let's just do it, and stop worrying so much."

Jake took a deep breath, calming himself. "Fine. Okay. What are you planning to do?"

"Well, we need to talk to Ptolemy. Cordelia said he lived in Gloucester, remember? I'll get the address from Cordelia and go up there to see him."

"Okay," Jake said, nodding. "Since you're taking the car, I think I'll stay at the manor and see if I can find anything in Cecil's room. We haven't done that yet. We should also look around the whole house, the abandoned part and all, to see if there are any clues that can help us."

"I agree," DeeDee said. "But if you do that while I'm gone, be careful. The place looks like it's rotting to the core. You might step on a floorboard that gives way, and you'll end up falling through the floor."

"Don't worry, I'll be careful," Jake said. "I'll ask Cordelia if there are any trouble spots."

"Just take care, okay?"

Jake laughed. "Now who's worrying?"

DeeDee grinned back at him.

When they got back to the manor, DeeDee changed out of her muddy boots and jeans and into an outfit more suitable for going to town. After speaking to Cordelia and getting Ptolemy's address, she gave Jake a kiss, grabbed her cell phone, put it in her purse, then took the car keys and left.

She followed the signs to Gloucester, noticing how beautiful the countryside was, but she couldn't enjoy it that much because she was concentrating so hard driving down the one-way lanes. "I'd never be able to get used to this," she said to herself out loud. To make things worse, the car was a stick-shift, when she was used to an automatic.

But soon, the tiny little roads led out onto a highway, and the drive through the rolling fields became much more enjoyable. The sun was bright, so she put on her sunglasses, and allowed herself to relax as she drove to Gloucester. It took just over a half hour.

Unexpectedly, she found Gloucester to be very green, with parks and trees just about everywhere she looked. Along with the modern buildings, there were historical stone ones that looked grand and gave the place a lovely atmosphere.

Soon she arrived at a large historical building with three stories and ornate detailing all over it. She thought it looked Victorian. There were a number of cars outside, so she assumed it was an apartment building.

She went inside and climbed the stairs to the top floor, surprised there wasn't an elevator. Cordelia had told her Ptolemy lived in a loft apartment, number 38. She soon found it, and knocked on the door, hoping everything would be all right. She memorized the numbers '999, not 911,' in case she got into trouble, slipped her cell phone into her pocket, and waited.

After a few moments, a very tall young man with tattoos on every spare inch of his skin opened the door.

"Are you Ptolemy Boatwright-Jones?" she asked.

He slammed the door in her face. "Who's asking?" he called from the other side.

"I'm... a friend of Cordelia's." She didn't want to say she was investigating, in case he didn't want to let her in.

"You're a liar," he said. "Cordelia doesn't have any friends."

DeeDee sighed. "All right. I'm not a friend exactly. But we're staying at Dockery Manor."

"Why would you want to stay there?" he asked in disgust.

She couldn't see any way around it. "My husband Jake and I are trying to find out what really happened to your grandfather."

There was a long silence, and then he opened the door. He looked at her for a long moment. "Are you with the CIA or something?"

DeeDee couldn't help but laugh. "I wish. Cordelia called us to help find out who killed Cecil, because the local police seem determined to prove that she was the one who killed him."

"Oh, okay. Well, she didn't do it. I know that." He stood to the side, gesturing for her to come in.

It was an absolutely lovely apartment, fresh and clean and bright. Because of the historical exterior, DeeDee had expected a place with wood paneled walls and antiques and dusty wall tapestries, kind of like Dockery Manor. But the apartment had been beautifully renovated with smooth white walls and dark wooden flooring. The overall feeling was a sleek and modern area.

He noticed her looking around and said, "My girlfriend Kelsey bought the furniture and chose the art."

"Well, she certainly has good taste," DeeDee said.

"Would you like a cup of tea?" he asked as they walked through the small hallway into the kitchen where every single surface was white and gleaming. "Or perhaps coffee? I don't think Americans drink tea much, do they?"

DeeDee flashed him a smile. "Not as much as the Brits. A coffee would be wonderful." In spite of her initial feelings, she was starting to warm up to him. She always tried not to warm up to suspects, because it could cloud her judgment, but despite his tattoos and intimidating look, there was something about him that made her feel at ease. She couldn't quite put her finger on why, but he just felt like a 'Good Person' to her, like his heart was in the right place.

She sat down on one of the white leather barstools at the marble kitchen island. "I'm sorry about your grandfather."

Ptolemy put the kettle on, then turned back to her and shrugged. "Thanks. He had a lot of years."

"Yes, but... well, he still went before his time."

"Hmm. That may be true, but you won't see much of an outpouring of sympathy for him, given the way he liked to treat everyone." DeeDee noticed that Ptolemy's words didn't match his demeanor. His eyes were filling with tears, and he quickly turned away to fix the coffee.

"What was your relationship with him like?" DeeDee asked gently.

"He was a horrible old man," Ptolemy said. "Well, he was always horrible, not just when he was old, so he was just a horrible man. But are any of us perfect?"

"No, that's certainly true," DeeDee said. "I've heard from a lot of people that he used to put people down and use abusive language. Did he do that to you?"

"Yep." He turned and grinned, although DeeDee saw a hint of sadness in his eyes. "But I did it right back to him. It used to make him angry, but I think he respected me for it. He seemed to enjoy my company, and whenever I said I had to leave, he'd pick another argument with me, to make me stay. We argued about everything from politics to family issues." He brought over her coffee and set it down in front of her.

"Thank you," DeeDee said with a smile. "It sounds like you went over there often."

"Yes, I did."

"Why's that, if he was so abusive?"

"Well, he was my grandfather, plus, I felt sorry for him, because nobody liked him, and I wanted to see Cordelia, my aunt. I also did some of his accounting work for him," he said. "But mainly it was about family ties. As I said, Cordelia has no friends to speak of, and I was worried about them getting lonely."

"That's kind of you," DeeDee said. "I'm sure you're busy."

"Sort of," he said. "But since I'm self-employed, I can set my own hours."

"Yes, I'm self-employed, too."

He brightened up. "Really? What do you do?"

"I run a catering business with a friend of mine. We cater a lot of high-end events and do a lot of different cuisines from around the world, fusions, that sort of thing."

"Aha," he said. "Excellent. It's wonderful being a business owner, isn't it?"

DeeDee smiled. "I do like it, although sometimes it can be stressful."

"But the money makes it worth it!" He sipped his cup of coffee, his eyes watching her over the top of the rim.

"Sometimes it is, sometimes it isn't," she said. "But that's especially true of my husband's business. He owns a private investigating firm. That's why we're here."

Ptolemy grinned. "You're contracting for him."

"Something like that," DeeDee said. "I've always wanted to see more of Europe, so..." She quickly caught herself. He put her so at ease, she realized she was getting too familiar with him, but maybe it was a good thing. If she opened up, maybe he would. "So... do you have any idea who could have killed your grandfather?"

Ptolemy's eyes became sad again. "I can see why they think Cordelia did it, or maybe even my father. Cordelia's very gentle and wouldn't even say boo to a goose, so my grandfather was very trying for her. And as for my dad..." He made a face which showed he was not a fan of his father.

DeeDee didn't say anything, waiting for him to elaborate.

"Let's just say my father is quite like my grandfather was, but doesn't want to admit it. They hated each other."

"I hesitate to ask this, but do you think your father could have killed your grandfather?"

Ptolemy looked thoughtful. "I've thought about it, but I've decided probably not. My father moved on many years ago. If he was going to kill my grandfather, he'd have done it a long time ago."

"But revenge is a dish best served cold, maybe...?"

"Maybe, but I doubt it," Ptolemy said, beginning to sound annoyed. "And the reason I doubt Cordelia did it was because she wasn't even sure the money was coming to her. Grandfather liked to frustrate her by telling her he was leaving all his money to a cat rescue home. He hated cats."

DeeDee didn't want to say anything, but just the thought of that made her feel very antagonistic toward Cecil. It seemed like emotional abuse to her - for Cecil to let Cordelia think she was less important to him than rescue cats, when he didn't even like cats.

"He told me in private he was joking and she'd get the money, because he didn't want it to go out of the family," Ptolemy said. "I told Cordelia that, but she said I was naive to believe it, and doing such a thing was totally in keeping with something he'd do. But she did get the inheritance. She just has to prove that she's innocent before she gets anything."

"Yes," DeeDee acknowledged. She wondered if Cordelia really had known she'd get the money. Surely, she could have gone through her father's things when he was asleep to find his will. It didn't seem like something Cordelia would do, but then again, in a murder investigation, what was ever as it seemed? "So, who do you think could have done it?"

"Pat Ives," he said immediately.

"The caregiver?"

"Yes." He had on an expression of absolute hatred on his face when he said her name.

"Why do you say that?"

"I don't have any evidence, so that's why I haven't gone to police about it," he said. "I haven't told anyone but you and my girlfriend. That woman... ugh... she just... gives off bad vibes."

DeeDee nodded. "If only bad vibes were enough for a conviction."

"Indeed."

"Just one thing, though. Sometimes those kinds of instinctual feelings are correct. For example, someone might meet a serial killer who is perfectly kind and pleasant, but just have a feeling something is wrong."

"I feel exactly like that."

"But also, you might have a bad feeling about someone because you have anxiety, or for a totally different reason. Maybe they remind you of someone from the past who did something to you, for example. So I don't think it can always be relied upon. I believe a lot of it is confirmation bias.

"You know, like you thought badly about three people and one of them turns out to have done something terrible, but the other two are innocent. You'd still say, I had a feeling about them and you'd be right, but you didn't take into account the other two instances when you were wrong."

"I don't know about all that," Ptolemy said. "I'm not really a person who gets hunches or whatever. My girlfriend's more into that stuff. But with this woman, there's something. Even when she smiles at me or says hello, it makes my skin crawl. I don't even want to be in the same room with her. You know what? I'll bet you a hundred thousand pounds she did it."

"Wow," DeeDee exclaimed. "You sound really firm in your conviction."

"I am," he said. "And, the truth is..." He looked down at the floor, then looked up again, sighed deeply, and looked into DeeDee's eyes. "I do care. Everyone hated my grandfather, except me. I've felt powerless to do anything about it. I just let it pass and said I would never go to that house again.

"I couldn't even tell Cordelia what I thought, because she's so grateful to Pat for taking care of grandfather for free. She wouldn't hear a word spoken against her. I know that, because I told Cordelia I didn't like her, way before grandfather died, and she told me not to be so unkind."

"So you've felt this way about Pat for a long time?"

"Yes, from the first time I laid eyes on the woman."

"Okay."

"But..." Unexpectedly, he choked back tears. "But you coming here, and doing this, it's woken me up. Maybe I can do something to help and get justice for grandfather. I want to set up a trap for her, or something. You know, get a confession from her."

"Slow down," DeeDee said quickly. "Let Jake and me do our investigation first. I promise we'll look into her all we can."

"Don't get taken in by her," Ptolemy warned. "She's very charming. She acts kind and nice, but she's a snake. An evil snake, underneath all that charm. Be careful."

"I will," DeeDee said. "I promise. I'd better get back now, but let me give you our cell numbers. I would have given you a business card, but of course those have our numbers in the States. One second." She rummaged in her purse, brought out a pad and paper, and wrote her phone number and Jake's down.

"Call us if you need anything. We'll keep you updated. But please don't do anything to Pat or even contact her. If she did do it, you don't want to give her a heads up you suspect her."

"Okay," Ptolemy said. "I won't." He took the slip of paper from DeeDee and put it in his pocket. Then he gave her an awkward hug. "Thank you for doing this for him," he whispered.

"Our pleasure," DeeDee said. "See you, Ptolemy."

He smiled. "Please, call me Toll."

CHAPTER TEN

On the drive back to Little Dockery, DeeDee had to wipe her mind clear. It was an unusual concept, but something she'd learned was absolutely crucial as an investigator. She'd told Jake about it, but he didn't have the same problem. DeeDee's problem was this...

She was an absolute lover of people. She adored people. She got a feel for people very quickly, and was usually very empathetic with whatever was going on with them. She wanted the best for them. She felt a little hurt when people told her their difficult experiences, and if they cried in front of her? She usually had a tear slide down her own cheek when they did.

It was a great trait to have when one was making friends. Cassie would attest to the fact that DeeDee was one of the best friends anyone could ever have, thoughtful and kind and full of empathic warmth.

It was also good when she was investigating a case, because it put people at ease. It made people trust her. It made them open themselves up to her and become more vulnerable, just like Ptolemy had done.

But it had one major drawback: It made DeeDee like people too much!

She understood almost everyone's side of the story. She could empathize with almost anyone's feelings. And any sly, manipulating predator who had murdered and wanted to get away with it could probably see this within her and use it to their advantage. They'd give her a sob story, and she'd buy into it and end up feeling sorry for them.

But over time, DeeDee had learned her natural gift had this downside, and she'd come up with a way to deal with it. She called it wiping her mind clear. And when she did it, she'd pick apart everything that happened, and make sure she saw it all from an objective view.

So, with Ptolemy, when she'd been in his kitchen, drinking his coffee, she'd believed everything he'd said. She assumed he'd been sincere. In fact, she'd felt his sincerity.

But when she was in the car, listening to some soft jazz as she cruised down the highway, she forced herself to stop feeling warmly toward him, and be more objective. Did he say anything suspicious? Perhaps. Questions came up for her like...

Maybe he was only around his odious grandfather so he'd be named in Cecil's will and get his money instead of Cordelia? And then he killed him to activate the will? But something went wrong somewhere...? Or maybe he knew that Cordelia would give him money if he asked for it...?

This would make sense. Perhaps that was the reason he was able to deal with Cecil's twisted nature.

Or...

Perhaps he was taking money from Cecil already... through the accounts? When that idea came into her head, it went ping like a lightbulb turning on. She called Jake on her hands free cell phone.

"Hey Jake!" she said, as soon as he answered his phone. "I've talked to Ptolemy, and he mentioned he did some of Cecil's accounts. I think we should get a forensic accountant to go over them to check and see if he's been siphoning off some of Cecil's money or anything like that."

"Good idea," Jake said. "What did you think of him?"

"At first he comes across as hostile and uncaring about his grandfather. I'd say just kind of matter-of-fact about him. Then he warmed up and told me he does care, and he has a suspect in mind."

"Really? Who?"

"Pat Ives, Cecil's caregiver," DeeDee said. "He basically said she's always given him the heebie-jeebies."

"Any specific reason?"

"Unfortunately not, although it would make sense, given that she was his caregiver. She'd be used to giving injections and of course, she had access to him all the time."

"Yes, definitely, but we've been told it happened at night when she wouldn't have been around," Jake said. "Although it's highly likely she had keys, or knew how to get in the house."

"Yes. I think we should talk to her next. I want to see if she has the same creepy effect on me."

"Me, too. We'll do this one together," he replied.

"Get anywhere with looking around the manor?"

"Not really. I bet I went into close to a hundred rooms, and there may be something interesting in some of them. There's a locked filing cabinet that felt heavy when I rocked it, so maybe it could have some papers of interest. Cordelia went to town for groceries, so when she comes back, I'll ask her if she has a key to it. I tried calling her cell phone, but she didn't pick up. Otherwise everything is just full of dust and decay. I picked up a teddy bear in one room and its head fell off!"

DeeDee laughed. "That's awful. You'll probably be scarred for life."

"Not quite, but I may need some therapy," Jake said with a laugh. "I don't mean to be judgmental, but I don't know how Cordelia lives like this. It can't be good for one's mental health."

"Well, she does look kind of depressed," DeeDee said. "It's probably the house as well as her father. It's such a big responsibility. You'd need a whole team to take care of everything."

"I'm sure she'll hire people to help her once she gets her inheritance," he said. "How far away are you? What shall we do next?"

"I'm about fifteen minutes away," she replied. "I'm starving, but I'm also very curious about Pat. If Cordelia's not there, shall we take a walk into the village, have lunch in the pub, and find out where Pat lives?"

"Sounds like a plan to me," he said. "I've got to shower to get this dust off me, and then I'll be ready. All this searching around has made me hungry, too."

*****

A little while later, Jake had showered and they began their walk into the village.

"Could you ever live somewhere like this?" DeeDee asked.

Jake grimaced. He looked around. "Well, it is beautiful," he said, gesturing at a nearby field and woodland. "But it's very isolated, and I don't even want to think what these tiny country roads are like when it snows."

"That's a very good point," DeeDee said. "I think you'd be pretty much stranded, unless you had a huge SUV with snow chains. I imagine Cordelia has to stay inside, or walk to the village to get supplies."

"Yes, I'm sure you're right," he said. "I think life would pretty much grind to a halt. Not only that, but the manor must be freezing. To heat the whole thing would cost an absolute fortune."

"I rather doubt it even has central heating," DeeDee said. "I think the dream of living in an English country manor sounds wonderful, but when you really think about it, it's not an easy life, is it?"

"No, I'd say more a labor of love. At least for Cordelia."

They continued talking about this and that and soon reached the center of the village. They passed an elderly man wearing corduroy trousers and a well-worn knitted sweater, with a tiny little dog on a leash.

"Hi there," DeeDee said.

"Oh, hello! American tourists?" the man asked. "How are you finding it here?"

"Yes, we're here for a visit," Jake said. "We love the English countryside."

The man beamed, as if he had designed the countryside himself. "Wonderful," he said. "Things have changed a lot around here, although most people still don't lock their doors. We never used to have a post office, and the pub is now run by Georgia Hay. Her parents used to run it, and she serves hot meals every single day. She even does a roast on Sundays and people come in from other villages. Can you imagine? It does something dreadful to the traffic, but we're proud of our Little Dockery Arms."

"Ah!" DeeDee said. "It sounds wonderful. We're actually going there for lunch. Anything special you'd recommend?"

"Well, they do a good Thai curry. But myself, I'm partial to the classics. They have steak and kidney pie. Oh, and toad in the hole."

"I've never heard of that before!" DeeDee said. "I presume it's not actual toads?"

The elderly man winked. "You'll just have to order it and find out!"

They all laughed. "We'll report back, if we see you," Jake said.

"We were also wondering... do you know where Pat Ives lives?"

The elderly man's face broke into a warm smile. "Of course. Just over there." He pointed across the street to a little row of higgledy cottages. "Number four, the one with all the flower baskets hanging outside. She's a lovely lady. Are you involved with the church?"

"No," DeeDee said. "We wanted to talk to her about Mr. Boatwright-Jones."

"Oh, him!" the man said derisively. "He always thought he was too good for the village. Treated us all like peasants, and he was lord of the manor. Pat was a saint for putting up with him. And she didn't get paid a penny, you know. Did it all out of the goodness of her heart."

"She seems to be a very generous woman," Jake said.

"Oh, yes. Raised her boys beautifully, helps with the church, teaches flower arranging, and makes the most beautiful arrangements. She also bakes bread for me regularly. She comes by quite often and drops off a fresh loaf for me. She's a gem of a woman."

"Wow," DeeDee said. "Sounds like she's very community-spirited."

"She's touched many a heart around here," the elderly man said. "So much so that many people forget she wasn't born here. It's her husband Michael who's the Little Dockery native. I'm sure she'll make you feel very much at home."

Jake smiled. "She sounds wonderful."

"That she is."

"Well, thank you, Mr... ?"

"Ken, call me Ken," he said. "And this is my dog, Opal."

DeeDee and Jake had both been looking down from time to time and smiling at the little thing, but she didn't seem to take much notice. She just wound herself around her owner's legs, obviously very attached to him. DeeDee could see she wouldn't enjoy being petted, so she didn't attempt it.

"Well, hello there, Opal. I'm DeeDee, and this is my husband Jake."

"Have a wonderful time. I hope England treats you well," Ken said with a smile, then made his way on through the village.

When he was out of earshot, Jake said, "This Pat woman sounds too good to be true."

"That's exactly what I was thinking," DeeDee agreed. "I'll bet she's hiding something."

Jake chuckled. "When exactly did we become so cynical? When did we decide that nobody could just be a good person?"

"When you opened your private investigator business," DeeDee said with a grin, poking him. "Now, let's go meet her, and find out if she really is some kind of Mother Theresa clone, or if she has any dark secrets she's hiding."

"Or skeletons in the closet," Jake added as they crossed the street. "Quite literally."

CHAPTER ELEVEN

Pat Ives answered the knock on her front door (which was so low one would have to duck to get through it, even DeeDee, who was quite short), with a large smile. "Ah!" she said, before they'd even opened their mouths. "You must be the Americans staying at Dockery Manor, DeeDee and Jake, I believe."

That made them open their mouths. "Yes!" DeeDee said, clearly shocked. "How did you know?"

Pat had a very pleased look on her face, like the cat that ate the cream. "I make it my business to know everything that's going on around here, my dear DeeDee. Do come in."

"Thank you," DeeDee said. "Actually, we wanted to invite you out, if that's all right. We were heading to Little Dockery Arms."

A flash of annoyance passed over Pat's face. It was so quickly there and gone that most people wouldn't have even noticed, but DeeDee, with her investigating prowess, picked up on it. She wondered why... because DeeDee and Jake had taken control, and were no longer on her turf? Or maybe she was just the hostess type, and always liked to lavish attention on guests at her home. Who knew? DeeDee would have to find out.

Pat fixed her face into a warm smile. "Oh, yes, that would be absolutely lovely. Let me just get my jacket and handbag. One moment." She disappeared into another room in the cottage, and quickly returned wearing a light jacket and carrying a tote bag that could hardly be called a handbag. She also had a fresh coat of dark pink lipstick on. "Off we go then," she said with a bright smile.

They walked the short distance to the pub. From the outside, the building was totally historical and fit in with the rest of the village. But inside, it was completely different. Although the original beams were there, they'd been painted in a light gray to complement the gray-topped tables, and gray velvet-padded chairs.

The walls were white, and there were mauve and pale pink accents around the pub. There were beautiful fake flower arrangements in pink, mauve, white, and silver, in sparkly pink vases. The place was dripping with stereotypical femininity.

The hostess stand at the front was unmanned, but Pat picked up three menus and led them inside. "We don't want to trouble anyone, do we?" she asked. There were only two elderly ladies at another table, dressed up as if coming out to a pub lunch was a grand affair. There were no other patrons. Pat waved to a young blond woman behind the bar. "Hi, Kelly! How's the family?"

"Hi, Pat! They're well, thank you! What about you and yours?"

"Brilliant, thank you! My little prince Noah can say his whole alphabet now. Oxford University had better watch out." She laughed, and they continued on to a table near the window. "I always like to sit by the window and watch the world go by," she told them.

Sure you do, DeeDee thought. *To make sure you don't miss a single happening in the village!*

Pat cocked her head on one side. "Is that okay with you?"

"Yes," Jake said. "It's better with the natural light."

That was true enough. The ceilings were very low, and going any farther into the pub would probably have made them feel claustrophobic.

Kelly came over to take their drinks order. "The usual, Pat?" she asked.

"Oh, yes, please," Pat said. "It's a bit naughty with lunch, but seeing as I've got these fine visitors from America, perhaps it's worth a bit of a celebration!"

"Oh! You're from America!" Kelly said, then put on an accent. "How totally awesome!"

It took everything DeeDee had to put on a smile and laugh a little.

"My friend from college, Rebecca, went to the United States. Her name's Rebecca Hunt. Do you know her?"

DeeDee died a little inside. "The United States is a big country, so I'm afraid we don't."

"Oh, okay. What a shame. She was a very nice girl," Kelly said. "What can I get you in the way of drinks?"

"I'll have a Diet Coke, please," DeeDee said.

"Hmm... I think I'll have the same," Jake said.

"Okay, great," Kelly said, and went back behind the bar.

"You've got a lovely modern man, haven't you?" Pat said to DeeDee in a stage whisper. "Diet Coke! He probably does the vacuuming and washes the dishes too, does he?"

"Indeed I do," Jake said. "We both work very hard running our businesses, so it only makes sense we share the workload at home."

"Ooh, you lucky girl," Pat said. "My Michael can't boil water, much less an egg or some such. As for cooking a meal? He wouldn't know where to start!" She rolled her eyes. "Men, hey? Absolutely useless."

"Hmm," DeeDee said. "Yes, I do know some men shy away from housework."

"I couldn't bear Michael intruding on that anyway," Pat said. "I like everything just so. He wouldn't do it the way I like it done."

DeeDee nodded.

Pat tapped Jake on the knee. "Don't worry, dear. I'm sure you do it wonderfully." It was a very patronizing statement. As Pat glanced out the window, Jake and DeeDee shared a meaningful look. Neither of them was warming up to Pat Ives.

"So..." Pat said. "I didn't know Cordelia was starting to take tourists up at the manor. I would have thought things needed to be... shall we say fixed up, first."

"Actually, our room is very comfortable," DeeDee said.

Pat smiled. "Oh, that's good. So, of all the lovely hotels in the Cotswolds, why on earth did you choose Dockery Manor?"

DeeDee supposed word would be getting around anyway. "We're actually not here for a vacation. We're here to investigate a little more into what happened to Cecil Boatwright-Jones."

"Oh," Pat said. She still smiled, but a sad shadow cast over her face. "Yes, to get justice for him."

"Yes," Jake said. "To get to the bottom of what really happened."

Kelly brought over their drinks - Pat's was a rosé wine spritzer - and they thanked her. She said she'd be back in a moment to take their food orders.

Pat nodded. "I'm glad you're here to help. Our local police force is wonderful. I'd never say a word against the police, but the more hands on deck, the better, I always say. Do look at the menu. What do you think you'll have?"

"We met a kind gentleman outside," Jake said. "Ken. He recommended the toad in the hole, and seeing as I've never had it…"

"And don't even know what it is!" DeeDee added.

"Neither do you," Jake said with a laugh. "And you're in the food industry!"

"Touché," DeeDee said. "Well, all that's about to change, since I'm going to order it, too."

"Ah, well, you're in for a treat," Pat said. "It's one of my favorites, but I'm watching my weight at the moment, so I'm going to opt for soup instead."

They put their menus down, and Pat sipped at her spritzer.

"You said you always like to know what's happening in the village," DeeDee ventured. "I suppose this means you'd have a lot of information about who could have… harmed Cecil?"

"Well…" Pat shifted in her chair. "I'm hesitant to speculate, because this is real life. I do watch murder mysteries on the television. Miss Marple, Midsomer Murders, and the like. The murders always seem to happen in places quite like here, don't they?

"You know, small English villages, with tight-knit communities. I do notice the parallels, and I've been tempted to do some investigating of my own, but Michael reminds me this is not television. He says the only appropriate thing to do is grieve, not investigate."

DeeDee was taken aback by the word grieve. It seemed like a very strange word to use. "Were you very close with Cecil?"

"Yes," she said. "I couldn't help but be, since I spent so long caring for him. It was five years, most every day, apart from when I taught my flower arranging class or went to see my sons and my grandchildren. For numerous hours a day."

"That's a long time to spend around someone," Jake agreed. "We've heard he had a somewhat... difficult character. Didn't that affect you?"

She laughed. "Oh, heavens, no. He intimidated others with his cruel jibes, but I understood right away what he was all about. As they say, sticks and stones may break my bones, but words will never hurt me.

"I never took any of his nonsense to heart. He soon realized that and toned it down quite a bit. He just needed someone with a firm but caring manner, and I was glad to be able to give him that."

DeeDee nodded. "You seem to have a knack for taking care of people."

"I was a nurse," Pat said proudly, "before I got married and had my boys."

Kelly came over and smiled. "Have you had a chance to look at the menu yet? What would you like to eat?"

Jake and DeeDee ordered toad in the hole with carrots, peas, and onion gravy, while Pat ordered a carrot soup with a whole wheat roll.

"You were saying you were a nurse," Jake said. "Was that locally?"

"Oh, no," Pat said. "Actually, quite far away from here. I moved here when I got married to Michael. He's from here, and I fell in love with the village. You wouldn't actually know it, but I'm from a large town. I never knew quiet country life growing up, but when I moved here, I realized I was definitely suited for it.

"I was very sad to leave my job, but I'd always wanted to be a housewife, so I decided to take up that role, and I became pregnant shortly after we were married. I never went back to nursing, since I wanted to be at home for my boys when they were young, and be there when they came back from the village school.

"I did miss it, but I knew my boys needed me. I still have a keepsake box from my time as a nurse. I was a pediatric nurse, mostly working with special needs children. It was a time in my life that I treasure very much."

DeeDee couldn't help it - she was beginning to warm up to Pat.

Pat became thoughtful. "Perhaps that's why Cecil's outbursts didn't affect me. A few of the children on the ward were difficult, but I knew instinctively they didn't know what they were doing, and needed understanding, care, and support, despite how unpleasant they were being."

She smiled sadly. "I suppose that stood me in good stead for Cecil's temper," she said with a sigh. "I didn't blame him, poor man. He lost his wife many years ago, so he must have been dreadfully lonely. He couldn't walk very well, and he disliked riding in a car, so he never really went anywhere.

"I tried to walk him around the grounds, but even with a cane and my help, he just didn't have the stamina for it. He categorically refused to use a wheelchair and physically assaulted me when I tried to get him into one, so he was cooped up in that room, and it was a dreadful old room. It was very cold and drafty until I absolutely insisted he install a fan heater. I think most people would find it difficult to be cheerful living in those circumstances."

"That's a good point," Jake said.

"Hmm," DeeDee said. She didn't mention what she'd heard about Cecil, that he'd always been nasty, way before his health declined.

"Confidentially, between us," Jake said, "do you have any ideas about who might have killed Cecil?"

Pat took a long, slow sip on her spritzer. "I will only talk if you absolutely promise you will keep this confidential. I may well be reading into things far too much. It may be a red herring, as they say on those mystery programs... Oh, I don't know if I should say anything."

DeeDee knew the best thing to do was to be quiet at this moment, and wait for the information to spill out.

"Fine, I will say it, but you really mustn't repeat it."

"We won't," Jake said.

DeeDee shook her head. "Not to a soul."

"I haven't even told the police yet," she said. "Perhaps I should, but... well, Cordelia is so fond of him, and one never knows..."

DeeDee's mind raced. John? Ptolemy?

"I sometimes suffer from the most dreadful insomnia. On the night of the murder, I was up in the kitchen, having a cup of tea and reading a book, hoping it would make me sleepy. It is deathly quiet in the village at that time of night, as you can imagine. I heard a very loud engine, like one of those posh sports cars, approaching. I went to the window and looked out, waiting for it to pass, and it was absolutely, 100%, Ptolemy Boatwright-Jones' car. He has a purple Maserati. You just cannot miss it. So... why was he traveling up to the manor in the middle of the night? That's very unusual for him."

"That's very useful information," DeeDee said. "Thank you for telling us. Don't worry, we won't repeat it."

"Thank you," Pat said, looking uncomfortable. "I'd hate for him to be implicated, if it was nothing. I mean, I've never known him to be up there so late, but maybe he had a reason for it. I don't want to be a part of someone innocent being suspected."

"We understand," Jake said.

DeeDee and Jake asked her more information about what she'd seen, and soon their meals arrived.

"Oh!" DeeDee said. "So, toad in the hole is sausages in batter!" She laughed. "No actual toads, thank goodness. Not even frogs."

"Frogs?" Pat said. "We're not like the French. It makes me squirm to even think of eating frogs!"

"I thought that, too," DeeDee said, "until I tried frogs' legs. They were absolutely delicious!"

Pat shuddered, then smiled. "Each to their own, dear. I think I'll stick to my carrot and coriander soup."

DeeDee and Jake thoroughly enjoyed their meal, but didn't learn much more from Pat. She told them a lot of things, about the village and the people who lived in it, and her beloved grandsons, but none of them were relevant to the investigation.

When they parted, Pat gave each of them a friendly pat on the shoulder. "Thank you for taking me out to lunch. What a treat! You're an absolutely lovely couple, and I wish you all the best. I hope you find out who killed poor Cecil and they spend the rest of their life in prison. Murderers are scum of the earth, and I wish they'd lock them all up and throw away the keys."

"We'll do our very best," DeeDee said. "We're determined to get justice for Cecil."

Pat nodded. "Good. Take care now."

They said their goodbyes, then DeeDee and Jake began walking back to Dockery Manor.

As soon as they'd turned the corner, Jake said, "What did you think of her?"

"Hmm... to be honest, I'm not sure," DeeDee replied. "She's nice and kind, but is there something more under the surface? My gut feeling is yes, but I can't say for sure."

"I had the same feeling," he said. "Like she's not quite as nice and kind as she first appears, but that doesn't necessarily make her a murderer. I think I'd be more suspicious if she was absolutely perfect and loving and giving. I'd say she was hiding her dark side too well. She does hide hers, but it's still visible, if you know what I mean."

DeeDee laughed. "We should have been psychoanalysts rather than investigators."

"We're forensic psychologists," Jake said with a wink.

"Though totally untrained!"

"Sadly, yes," Jake said.

"I wouldn't mind going back to school to do something like that. I know people think it's silly to do that at my age, but I don't think so. The way things are going with you - Mr. Adventurer - I think we'll be solving cases well into our 70's."

"Mr. Adventurer!" Jake said with mock-outrage. "And you just come along on my adventures out of a sense of duty but hating every moment. Would I be right?" His eyes sparkled with mischief.

DeeDee smirked. "Something like that."

"Ha! I'm doing this for business, and you admit you're doing it for pleasure. What does that say about you?"

"Oh, all right, all right, you got me," DeeDee said. Her thoughts became more serious. "As I said, we really do need to get a forensic accountant on the case. Let's take care of that when we get back."

"Okay," Jake said. "I'll take care of it."

"Good," DeeDee said. "I'm wondering if there's any way we can verify Pat's story about Ptolemy's car without letting him know that we might consider him to be a suspect. Maybe surveillance?"

"Doubtful around here," Jake said. "Although..." He looked back down the street. "The post office may have security cameras. Let's go back and check there."

DeeDee nodded. "Good idea."

CHAPTER TWELVE

Jake and DeeDee walked back toward the Little Dockery Post Office, looking for any signs of cameras.

"Yes, look, right there!" DeeDee said excitedly when they got to the front of the tiny little store. There was a small camera perched underneath the low eave of the cottage-style building that would probably capture a little of the street as well as the front door of the Post Office.

They went inside through a very small glass door, and a little bell rang to announce their entrance.

There was no one in the cramped store, not behind the cash register, and not in the tiny little aisles between shelves. The Post Office, they soon discovered, was a cashier space in a small convenience store, and consisted of a digital scale to weigh parcels. That was all.

"One sec!" a young female voice hollered from somewhere they couldn't see behind the shelves. They heard the thud of someone coming down the stairs, and heard the swing of a door in the far corner, which was well-hidden by numerous shelves.

"Hiya, sorry for the wait," the young woman said as she came into view. She looked to be in her twenties, with a very messy dishwater-blond bun on top of her head, thick rimmed glasses, and a baby on her hip who was in a white onesie. She looked exhausted.

"Hello," DeeDee said with a warm smile.

"Who's this little one?" Jake asked.

The young woman smiled at them, then down at the little baby. "This is my little girl, Ruby." She switched to a baby voice. "Can you say hello, Ruby?"

Ruby watched DeeDee and Jake warily, then pushed her face into her mother's neck to hide from them. Her little frown was adorable. "Oh, she's precious!" DeeDee said. "My kids are all grown up now, and I miss those times."

The young woman grinned. "Bet you don't miss the sleepless nights, though, do you?"

"Ah, I'll give you that!"

"Nah, she's gorgeous," the young woman said, clearly feeling guilty. "Even if you do keep me up half the night, you little monster." She tickled Ruby, who collapsed into peals of cute baby giggles. "I'm afraid I'm going to freak you out now by knowing your names, since Ken came in and told me about you. DeeDee and Jake. I'm Anna."

"Hi, Anna," DeeDee said with a laugh. "We've kind of gotten used to people being ready for us before we arrive. It's such a close-knit community."

"I know!" Anna said. "I do love it here, but when I went away to uni it was such a culture shock. Nobody said hello, nobody knew me. Here, if you so much as brush your teeth, the whole neighborhood knows about it in five seconds flat."

DeeDee laughed. "That's quite something."

"So, were you looking for something in particular?"

"Well, we didn't come in for these, but they look like the perfect post-Toad-in-the-whole palate cleansers," Jake said, taking some chocolate and putting it on the counter. He looked to DeeDee for approval on his choice, and she nodded. "We noticed you had a surveillance camera outside. We're here looking into what happened to Cecil Boatwright-Jones, and there may be footage on the camera that could help us."

Anna grimaced. "I'm really sorry, but it's a dummy one. It doesn't record footage. It's not even hooked up. We just got it because once some boys from the next village came over and tried to steal from us, and it was a deterrent for them. They were just schoolboys, so we didn't feel like we needed to get anything that actually functioned. And no one in this village would ever steal from this shop, so..."

"Oh," DeeDee said, disappointed. "Well, never mind." Then she had an idea. "Wait a moment! On the night that Cecil died, were you up with Ruby at any time?"

"I'm up with Ruby in the night every night," Anna said with a weary smile, shifting Ruby onto the other hip as she began to fuss.

"Okay. Do you remember a loud vehicle passing up and down, in the night?"

"Hmm... no, I don't think so. Occasionally a vehicle will drive through the village late at night, but I can't remember any in particular. Honestly, I don't even know what I was doing the night Cecil was murdered. With this little one, all the nights... and the days... seem to blend into one at the moment."

"I can imagine," Jake said. "Well, please let us know if you remember anything. We're staying at Dockery Manor."

"Sure," Anna said. "That'll be one pound and eighty-three pence for the chocolate."

By the time they got back to the manor lane, the chocolate was long gone. They ambled up the street, talking about what they would do next - the finer details of the forensic accountant, and how they'd break the matter of cost to Cordelia. They wondered if they should go and see Richard Boatwright-Jones. Perhaps he'd be able to shed some light on Ptolemy.

Jake began, "I think that would be a good idea, and we can have a day trip to London. I really want to…"

But he stopped dead, staring straight ahead of him as they reached the fountain. His mouth dropped open.

DeeDee looked along his line of sight toward the manor.

"Oh!" she gasped.

Flames leaped out of the abandoned wing from the windows and from the roof. Ominous black smoke poured out of the windows and billowed darkly into the gray sky above.

Cordelia ran out the front door, screaming. "No! No!" She turned back to gape at the blazing wing. "No! My house!"

DeeDee thought quickly and pulled out her phone as they ran toward Cordelia. The heat hit her in the face like a flaming punch. Jake grabbed Cordelia and pulled her back. DeeDee called 911, and it just beeped. She kept trying over and over, in a panic, before realizing she was calling the wrong number.

"It's 999!" she yelled at herself. She punched in the number.

"Police, ambulance or fire service?" the operator answered.

"Fire! Fire!" DeeDee said.

Jake was desperately trying to hold Cordelia back as she screamed, trying to get closer to the house, as if she could stop it from burning. A complete frenzy had taken over her body as she screamed and screamed.

When she got through to the operator, DeeDee blurted out, "There's a huge fire at Dockery Manor in Little Dockery village. Come quick! It's raging!"

"I'll send out a fire crew now. Do not go in the building. Stay well away from the building. Electrics can catch fire and cause explosions."

"Okay," DeeDee said. With a powerful strength that seemed to come out of nowhere, she grabbed Cordelia's other arm, and took off toward the fountain, Jake having to catch up with Cordelia's other arm.

They finally got to the fountain, tugging against Cordelia's surprising strength, and once there, she crumpled, falling on Jake. They propped her up, and she stared at the manor house. "No," she kept saying, but now her voice was a whisper. "No. No."

DeeDee looked at the house and shook her head sadly.

"Where is the fire department?" Jake said. "It's taking them so long to get here."

DeeDee looked at her phone. To her astonishment, she'd only called them three minutes ago. It felt like at least a half hour had gone by. Every second those flames leaped was a second too long. All they could do was huddle together, in horror, watching as the abandoned wing burned, hoping and praying that the ravenous fire would spare the rest of the manor.

Eventually, seemingly eons later, they could hear the sound of the fire truck siren in the distance. DeeDee imagined it passing through the winding country lanes, and understood why it took so long. The roads were barely wide enough for it.

Finally it swung into the manor estate road, their red savior, with a blaring siren and flashing blue lights. They moved out of the way, and it sped past them, coming to an abrupt halt a little way in front of the house.

Firefighters in black suits with bright yellow hats and yellow tanks on their backs jumped out of the vehicle and rushed around at lightning speed, setting up hoses and running around the property, trying to get a better look at what was happening.

Soon the water was flowing from some regular hoses and from a high-pressure hose at the back of the truck. The smoke turned white, pouring out of the windows so thickly it shrouded the whole building. The water kept flowing, and all DeeDee, Jake, and Cordelia could do was stand and watch, transfixed to the spot.

After what seemed like a long time, the smoke began to clear. The abandoned wing was revealed, and Cordelia broke down, sobbing.

DeeDee couldn't blame her. It was horrible. Huge black smoke stains surrounded the windows. Water was dripping everywhere from the abandoned wing. It was gutted, and from where they were standing, it looked as if the inside had been completely and totally charred.

One of the firefighters walked up to them. "Are you the owners?" he asked, taking off his helmet.

"I am," Cordelia said numbly.

"Okay," he said. "I'm afraid you're going to have to vacate the building for the time being. We have to check for any structural damage, and it's not safe to stay here. You'll need to make some alternative arrangements for accommodations."

Cordelia croaked, "I'm going to stay here."

The firefighter looked surprised. "I'm afraid you can't. I understand it's your home, but it may not be habitable. We really need to check it."

"I'll stay in the East Wing on the other side."

"I'm afraid I'm going to have to insist you vacate it," he said.

"Don't worry. It may be that it's fine to return to, but we need to make sure for your safety. I'd also advise you to call your insurance company and let them know about the fire."

Cordelia swallowed. "I don't have any insurance."

"Ah, I see." He looked sorry for her, and knew he couldn't say anything to help, so he came across as being awkward. "Well, I'd better get back to the crew. Let me know if you need anything."

Jake and DeeDee organized alternative accommodation for her. Farmer Killian and his wife Rosie agreed to let Cordelia stay as long as she needed to. A member of the fire crew escorted her into the hallway and the East Wing to get some of her belongings, and DeeDee was afraid she'd cling to one of the grand pillars and refuse to leave, but fortunately she didn't. She came out of the house moments later, looking like a ghost.

DeeDee and Jake weren't allowed up to their room. The staircase was out of use, and the room they'd been staying in was too close to the abandoned West Wing, so they had to leave with nothing. Thankfully DeeDee had taken her purse with her to town, which had her money, credit cards, phone, charger, the car keys, and both of their passports.

They looked online, and found a nearby boutique hotel that had space for a few days at a reasonable rate. In reality, it was six guest rooms above a pub, but the pictures and reviews showed it to be clean, comfortable, and recently redecorated.

They took a quick trip into town to buy pajamas, new clothes, toothbrushes, and some other things they'd need. They found a large store called Asda which had homewares, garden tools, televisions, and about anything else anyone could ever want, and all for extremely good prices.

The room they'd booked came with a free breakfast, but they bought some snacks and drinks just in case, and headed to it.

They were so busy they hadn't thought much about the fire, only about what they needed for that night. But once they were settled in their room, with their meager Asda bags of possessions, images began to flash into DeeDee's mind.

Jake was sitting on the bed, staring into space, and he sighed deeply. DeeDee knew he was picturing the exact same thing. "You're thinking about it, aren't you?" she said softly.

"Yes," he replied. "Poor Cordelia."

"She loves that place so much," DeeDee said. "That's not just her home, it's her ancestors' home. I can't even imagine how she must be feeling right now."

"And not to have any insurance..." Jake said. "I'm sure Cordelia would have gotten it as soon as the inheritance came through, although it would have been extremely expensive for such a historic, large building." He paused. "I imagine she decided to pay our fees instead of insuring it." He sighed even more deeply.

"Maybe, although you can't be sure of that," DeeDee said. "And if she did, that was her choice. I do feel sorry for her, though. Cecil must not have had any insurance on it, because if he had, I would think it would still be in force."

"You're right."

"The more I hear about him, the more I learn about his character," DeeDee said. "I'd bet everything I have that the reason he didn't insure it was because he knew Cordelia loved it so much. She'd probably begged him to do it."

"Maybe," Jake said. "Either way, he sounds like a very strange man. Even if that wasn't the case, and he just didn't like spending his money, surely your house is the first thing you insure. Didn't he care about his family's legacy?"

"I'm getting the sense that Cecil only cared about Cecil."

"This just makes it all the more urgent," Jake said. "We have to clear her name and help the police close the murder investigation, so she can get her inheritance and the money to fix it up."

"Yes," DeeDee agreed. "It's time to ramp up our investigation. No more time for casual lunches or leisure time in London. It's time to go full speed ahead."

CHAPTER THIRTEEN

Jake and DeeDee had a good, long sleep in the cozy hotel. Although their room at Cordelia's had been clean and comfortable, it had been very drafty and they woke up early, feeling very cold even though it was spring.

DeeDee slept a long time, and woke up to find Jake fully dressed and enjoying a continental breakfast. "Oh, that smells lovely!" DeeDee said sleepily, stretching, and yawning. "Why didn't you wake me up?"

Jake grinned. "I tried. You told me angrily that I'd let the cow out of the gate again, and I must be more careful in the future. Then you turned over and started snoring."

"I did not say that. Did I?"

"You did," he said with a chuckle. "Apparently you've seen too many fields in the last few days."

She laughed along with him. "Sorry."

He made an elaborate bow and put on a posh voice. "Doth madam desire breakfast in bed?"

"Madam doth indeed, you nutcase," DeeDee replied. She sat up and looked down at the breakfast tray. There was a coffeepot, a teapot, a pitcher of orange juice, a rack of toast triangles with little butter packets and mini jam jars, two croissants, two pain au chocolat, and two muffins that appeared to be blueberry. "Pass me a coffee and a pain au chocolat, would you, darling?"

He poured a coffee for her and passed the pain au chocolat on a little saucer.

"Thank you," she said.

"I've hired the forensic accountant, but I've got to find out if it's safe to go back inside the manor. I hope Cecil's account books didn't burn up."

"There must be electronic versions in this day and age," DeeDee said. "Surely they couldn't have had it only on paper. That would seem very old-fashioned." She bit into the pain au chocolat, which was surprisingly good. She'd encountered many poor, slightly stale continental breakfasts in her time, but this wasn't bad at all. The pain au chocolat was buttery, perfectly flaky, with the right amount of crunch, and still slightly warm. It was lovely.

"Yes, but I'm guessing only Ptolemy has access to them," Jake said.

"You're probably right. I can't see Cordelia knowing anything about them. Speaking of Cordelia, I wonder how she is this morning. Maybe I should go see her."

"Yes, I think you should." Jake said. "And you could find out whether we can get access to the accounts records."

"And our things from our room," DeeDee added. "I also want to find out if Ptolemy's car was seen by anyone else. If not, maybe Pat is the killer and trying to throw us off the scent with a false story. I'll go into the village and see what I can find out."

"Okay," Jake said. "I don't really want to make the drive, but I think I should go to London. I'll hire another car and head down there. It's still pretty early, so I could probably get back here by late tonight."

DeeDee frowned. "That's five hours' driving for the day. Are you sure?"

"Five hours is nothing!" he said. "We've done longer than that in one stretch."

"Yes, but that was in the U.S., and it was a lot more familiar to us."

"It will be fine, DeeDee, trust me. I'll look into renting one now," he said, taking his phone out of his pocket.

"I suppose it is crucial for you to get Richard's perspective on this." She thought of suggesting to Jake that he do it by phone, but she knew from what he'd told her and from her own personal experience, that nobody opened up on the phone in quite the same way. If you wanted the truth, you had to meet someone face to face. And if that meant five hours of driving, then so be it.

*****

Jake had predicted he'd make it to Richard's offices in London at around midday, taking into account a twenty-minute stop to buy a suit, dress shirt, and shoes, which he hoped would help him get through the door at Richard's office. He realized that had been wildly optimistic when he reached the M25 ring road that circled around London, and he got stuck in slow crawling traffic for over an hour. The road going into the city wasn't much better.

As for finding somewhere to park near Richard's offices? It was like finding a needle in a haystack. He drove around the same block about twenty times until he finally found a space, which was eye-wateringly expensive at £20 per hour. He promised himself he'd never complain about Seattle parking prices again.

102

They'd found out from Cordelia that Richard was a commercial tax lawyer and a senior partner at Minkin & Schroeder, one of the most prestigious firms, not only in London, but in the world.

Jake arrived at their headquarters and after fixing his collar and smoothing out his shirt, walked into the palatial entrance hall. He didn't call ahead to make an appointment, because he hadn't wanted to give Richard the opportunity to say no.

"I'm here to see Richard Boatwright-Jones. I'm a friend of his sister, Cordelia," he told the receptionist.

The receptionist made a call, got approval, and told Jake to write his name and time of arrival in the visitor's book. Then she handed him a visitor pass to put around his neck. "He's on the top floor." She gestured toward two golden elevators.

"Thank you," Jake said.

He rode up alone after punching number thirty, the highest number he could see. When the elevator door opened, he was in front of another receptionist, but this one had been alerted to his arrival. He was asked to sit in the waiting room, and after a short time, Richard Boatwright-Jones appeared from a door in the back.

Jake instantly knew it was him. He was tall like Cecil (Jake had seen photos of Cecil and Ptolemy) and Ptolemy, and had auburn hair like Cordelia. He was slimmer than Cordelia, but there was a definite resemblance between them. He looked at Jake with curiosity, and motioned for him to come into his office.

Jake stepped in, introduced himself, and shook Richard's hand. He took in the office, which was very modern and sleek, a whole different feel from the old-world grandeur of Dockery Manor.

Richard sat behind his desk and gestured for Jake to sit down. "I'm going to have a cup of coffee," he announced. "Would you like anything?"

"A coffee would do just fine for me too, thanks," Jake said. "Black, no sugar."

Richard nodded and called the receptionist to tell her what he wanted. Then he leaned back in his chair and interlaced his fingers. "You're a friend of Cordelia's, you say? That surprises me."

"Why's that?"

"Cordelia's always been more of a church mouse than a social butterfly," he said, some contempt in his voice. "How on earth did you meet her? The last I heard, she barely leaves that godforsaken manor."

"There was a fire there yesterday," Jake said.

Richard's demeanor instantly changed. His face flooded with concern. "Was she hurt?"

"No," Jake said. "She's absolutely fine. Well, obviously she's devastated. An entire wing burned, but she's not physically hurt, no."

Richard breathed a sigh of relief. "Thank goodness. It's a shame the whole manor didn't burn to a crisp, though." He furrowed his brow. "Where do you know her from?" he asked again.

"I'll be honest with you," Jake said. His investigative gut feelings were telling him to, and he'd learned to trust them. "The police seem to think she killed your father, and she hired my private investigating firm to find out who did it, so she could clear her name."

Richard got up from his chair, looked out of the panoramic window that had a breathtaking view of the London skyline, and thrust his hands in his pockets. "I see," he said with a smirk. "So, you've discovered my father and I were estranged, and you've decided to come poking about to see just how angry I am about it, to see if I could have been the guilty party."

"Not exactly, no. I'm not here to accuse you of anything."

Richard smirked again. "Then just to pry."

Jake just looked at him, and Richard sighed. "I do apologize. The sooner I hear nothing more about that wretched man or that wretched manor, the better."

Their coffees arrived, and they both thanked the receptionist. Jake broke the tension by saying, "Excellent coffee."

"Yes, I drink only a very specific Ethiopian blend. In my view, you can't get better."

"I may have to take down the name of it," Jake said. "I'm a big coffee drinker and this is just... hmmm... perfect."

Richard laughed, in spite of himself. "You're trying to butter me up, so I'll talk more. And it may even be working."

Jake smiled. "It's my job, sir. Sorry."

Richard got serious again. "Look, are you absolutely sure it's murder? It could have just been a mistake with medication, couldn't it?"

"The police are pretty convinced it was murder."

Richard grimaced. "Well... I don't know. I haven't been there in thirty years."

"That's a long time. You must have pretty strong reasons for not talking to your father for all that time."

"You bet I do," Richard said. "The man was... poison on legs. A devil who had somehow wrangled a spot on Earth in a human body."

"Wow. That's quite an indictment."

"It's my opinion."

Jake nodded. "And I'm sure for very good reason. Everyone who knew him has attested to his... temperament. Didn't you want to see Cordelia, though?"

"Yes, but in her words, she wouldn't see me because I'd turned my back on the family and lineage."

"She often talks of her ancestors and the history of the manor, but you don't seem as interested."

"I'm not in the slightest. Father held it to our heads like a gun, the money, the house. I refused to play his games, bowing and scraping so he wouldn't leave me out of his will. I don't need or want any of his money."

"You're not going to be inheriting anything?" Jake asked.

"No idea," Richard said. "And I'd send the money back to the estate if I did. Without meaning to be crude, I've made plenty of my own that isn't tainted with his cruelty."

"What about Ptolemy?"

Richard looked irritated. "What about him?"

"Will he inherit anything?"

"I don't know," Richard snapped. "You seem to be under the impression that I know all the ins and outs of this issue, when I haven't been around the man for three decades."

"Does Ptolemy give you updates?"

"Updates?" he sneered. "What on earth would I want those for? Ptolemy went to see my father semi-regularly, but that's none of my business whatsoever. He's a grown man. He can do whatever he wants."

"Does he come to see you often?"

Richard was getting increasingly irritated. "What does that have to do with anything?"

"I just thought..."

"No," Richard snapped. "No, you know what, this is just ridiculous. I don't know anything about my father or his death or any will or any inheritance. I have nothing to offer you, and an extremely long to-do list, so I'm going to ask you to leave and to direct any further questions you might have for me via email." He handed Jake a business card.

"All right," Jake said, standing up and putting the business card in his suit jacket. "Just one last thing..."

"What is it?" Richard asked tersely.

"I don't want to overstep the mark, but... like you said, you're a man with plenty of money. The manor's falling down, and now a whole wing has burned. That's where your sister lives. If I were you, I think I'd contribute to restoring the manor, even if just to make sure my sister was safe."

Richard smirked. "Oh you would, would you? Thank you for your most enlightening input. Goodbye."

Jake, frustrated, left. He went back down in the elevator cursing himself. He'd not been on top of his game form. Usually, he'd have done an off-the-cuff interview, but this time he'd prepared questions, and it had lacked the flow so necessary to these types of conversations.

He decided to go out and get a fast food meal to eat before he left London. He found a McDonalds, which he didn't eat very often, and bought himself a veritable feast to keep fortified for his drive back.

CHAPTER FOURTEEN

While Jake was on his London trip, DeeDee went to check up on Cordelia at Farmer Killian's, but when she got there, neither Cordelia nor Killian were there.

Rosie was outside feeding the chickens. "Oh, hello, lovey, you must be DeeDee," she said warmly. "Are you looking for Cordelia? She's gone up to the manor."

"Thank you," DeeDee said. "Was she all right?"

"Not really, love," Rosie said. "She cried all night, but that's to be expected. Poor thing has had a tough time of it lately."

"Yes, she has," DeeDee agreed.

"She wanted to see how the fire department was doing, and she left first thing this morning."

"I think I'll go over there now. Thanks. It's Rosie, isn't it?"

"That it is." She looked so much like a stereotypical English farmer's wife, with a ruddy face, warm smile, muddy boots, and an apron tied around her waist over her clothes, that it made DeeDee smile.

"Take care," DeeDee said, then got back in her car and headed over to Dockery Manor.

As she drove up the driveway, she looked at the manor and her heart sank. It looked even more depressing than ever, with the half-charred wing staring out at her with its windows looking like black, soulless eyes. On one hand, she admired Cordelia's commitment to her family history.

On the other, she wondered if she weren't fighting a losing battle. Maybe there was a very good reason most of these grand old mansions were bulldozed, converted into apartments, or placed in the care of the National Trust. They were just too large and unwieldy for a modern family to run without scores of servants.

But Cordelia was unperturbed. DeeDee found her in the hallway, whistling a happy tune, and dusting off the antiques with a bright turquoise feather duster.

"Hi, Cordelia. How are you?"

Cordelia spun around, a big smile on her face. "DeeDee!" she exclaimed.

DeeDee couldn't help but smile, too, although she was a little worried. "Everything okay?"

"More than okay!" Cordelia said. "Splendid. Absolutely marvelous, I'd say!"

"Why's that...?"

"Well, the whole manor didn't burn down, did it? And the firefighters have told me all the fire damage was confined to the West Wing. They've said I can move back in, and of course you can, too. Best of all, I'd moved all the family heirlooms out of the West Wing, so nothing of value was destroyed, and it can all be restored!"

"That is good news," DeeDee said. "Do they know what started the fire?"

"Faulty wiring," Cordelia said. "Some of the wiring is ancient, so that will all have to be redone as well, and I can't wait to begin. As soon as you and your husband prove I'm innocent, we can get started on the renovations right away." She clapped her hands. "I can just feel this is all going to work out fine. I'm sure the investigation is going swimmingly, isn't it?"

"We're following up a lot of lines of inquiry," DeeDee said. "Jake's in London right now talking to your brother."

"Brother?" Cordelia said. "If you mean Richard, you can forget it. He was my brother once, a long time ago. But not anymore."

"You've disowned him?"

"He disowned himself from the family," Cordelia said scornfully. "Now, I must get into the garden. John is arriving soon to spruce up the fountain."

"Okay," DeeDee said. "I think I'll look in Cecil's room, if that's okay. I know Jake gave it a onceover, but I'd like to comb through it myself."

"Be my guest," Cordelia said. "The whole house is open to you, except the West Wing, of course. The firefighters have blocked it off with boards and bright tape, so you won't stumble in there accidentally."

"Okay," DeeDee said. "Hope the fountain goes well, Cordelia."

Cordelia gave her a bright smile and a slightly patronizing look. "Of course it will."

DeeDee walked through the house to Cecil's room, which was actually a suite. It was in keeping with the rest of the house, old-fashioned, with dark paneled walls and thick Victorian curtains at the windows. Everything was covered with a very thin layer of dust, but underneath that it was clean. There were no years of encrusted grime like on the fountain.

It was actually furnished comfortably and warmly, though in a slightly outdated way, with pinks and beiges and pale greens, frilly pillows, and floral prints. There was a soft beige carpet on the floor that was totally luxurious.

But the strangest thing was, although DeeDee could see the warm, homely luxury with her eyes, she couldn't feel it.

DeeDee was a big believer that different places carried their own energy. She'd experienced it a few times. When house hunting, she'd found a beautiful home that had everything she'd wanted, but as soon as she'd stepped into it, every instinct in her had shouted, "No! No! No!"

She just knew, without having anyone tell her, that the last people who lived there had been very unhappy. And sure enough, she later found out the owners were selling due to a very acrimonious divorce.

She'd also gotten 'feelings' in historical places. And she got a 'feeling' now, and the feeling was anger. If walls could talk, she thought they'd be hissing snide, nasty remarks at her and telling her to get out.

It felt so strong, she almost turned on her heel and marched back out. But she stopped herself, and forced herself to look around the room, her eyes scanning every surface, hopefully finding something of interest.

"Maybe the accounting books will be in here?" she mused aloud to herself.

Apart from the layer of dust, it was all very neat and tidy. Suspiciously neat and tidy. There was absolutely no clutter around, nothing that showed signs of someone having lived there. She supposed since the killer had access to the room, they'd have also managed to hide everything. She suspected that any clues would be long gone.

She flopped down on a chair, feeling dejected. It felt like they were getting nowhere with the investigation. Nothing was clear or straightforward. And getting mixed up in all the family's business was emotionally tiring. Why did everything have to be so complicated, with estrangement, animosity, inheritance issues, and ancestors?

She sighed deeply, and it really sank in at that moment what was important more than anything – family. She couldn't wait to see her grown-up kids and wrap her arms around them. She got lost for a moment in pleasant reverie, reminiscing back to when her children were little.

A figure suddenly appeared in the doorway and practically made her jump out of her skin. She leaped to her feet. "Who on earth are you?" she asked, too rattled to think of manners.

The elderly, well-dressed man in the doorway furrowed his brow. "I think the question is, who on earth are you?" he asked, in a very posh accent.

DeeDee laughed nervously, trying to tell herself there was nothing to worry about. "I'm DeeDee Wilson. And you are?"

He strode into the room. "You're American, I presume?"

DeeDee took an instant dislike to him. Not only did he not answer her question, he acted like he didn't have to. Like he owned the room, or perhaps the whole world, and concepts like manners were far too lowly for him to take into account. "Yes," she said. "And you're, of course, British... Mr...?"

"What are you doing in Cecil's room?"

"What are you doing in Cecil's room? Does Cordelia know you're here?"

"Are you a new housekeeper?" he asked. He ran his finger along the sideboard. "If you are, you had better get your duster out, pronto."

He was obviously very skilled in making people feel small. Perhaps she was talking to Cecil, who had risen from the dead. She shook her head and put a smile on her face, went over to him and held her hand out. "I'm DeeDee Wilson, a private investigator looking into Cecil Boatwright-Jones' murder. And you are...?"

He looked at her hand warily, but obviously he couldn't be so rude as to leave her hanging. He gripped her hand with his cold, clammy one, and looked into her eyes. He was smiling, but his eyes were like those of a serpent. A shiver crept up DeeDee's spine, and she quickly extricated herself from the handshake.

"I am Walter Smythe," he said finally. "A very good friend and business partner of Cecil's. I'm visiting to check on Cordelia's welfare."

DeeDee nodded. "She's out by the fountain, isn't she? Didn't you see her? She seems very buoyant this morning."

"Yes, I did," he said, not offering any further explanation as to why he was in Cecil's room. He looked at her with an amused, patronizing smile. "Found any clues?"

"Nothing of interest," she said, making a mental note she'd have to come back and rummage through the drawers as soon as he'd left. "Except you!" She smiled. "Do you have any idea who would have wanted to kill Cecil?"

"None, none whatsoever," he said. "And I won't talk about the matter again. I find it a deeply insensitive question, and..."

"I understand," DeeDee said. "Unfortunately asking such things is part of my job description."

"Well, kindly keep your job and all the tasteless questions it entails away from me."

"That's a rather suspicious thing to say."

"So be it."

"Then you don't want to share anything with me that might serve as an alibi, or any information that could..."

"I will be sharing absolutely nothing with you," he said. "Go and find the housekeeper and tell them to make up a room for me. I'm staying here tonight."

DeeDee was surprised how quickly her annoyance morphed into absolute rage that thundered through her veins. "There isn't a housekeeper," she snapped, then quickly left the room, realizing she needed to cool down, and headed out the front door. She strode quickly toward the fountain, forcing herself to take deep, drawn-out breaths.

She found John and Cordelia scrubbing away at the moss and algae on the fountain.

"Well!" DeeDee said. "Do you know a so-called Walter Smythe who is here?"

"Yes," Cordelia said. She nodded towards the house, where a silver Bentley was parked on the driveway. DeeDee had been so incensed she hadn't even noticed it. "He's Daddy's great friend."

"He was extremely rude to me."

"Oh, yes, Walter has no manners, I'm afraid. Well, not towards anyone unless they're like him."

"Illuminati members," John mumbled.

"Don't be so utterly silly, John," Cordelia said, though there was a warm, soft tone to her voice. "No, unless you're an extremely wealthy man of a certain age, you're neither relevant nor respected. It's just his way."

He and your father were well-matched, DeeDee thought. "I see," she said.

But she hadn't yet experienced Walter Smythe's capacity for being boorish, rude, and while genteel in his manner, conveying extremely aggressive sentiments underneath.

She would experience it, and perhaps an even deeper treachery he held in his heart, that very night.

CHAPTER FIFTEEN

For some reason DeeDee didn't understand, Cordelia seemed very intent on making sure Walter Smythe was impressed. She laid out a huge afternoon tea spread for him, and was hopping all over the kitchen like a mad fly when DeeDee came in.

"Cordelia, do you know where your father's accounting books are?"

"Sorry, DeeDee, I don't," Cordelia said, not looking up as she frantically wiped off the fine china. "Daddy always said I was hopeless with numbers, and he was absolutely right. He always got Tolly to deal with them. Maybe Tolly has them himself, I'm not sure."

"Oh, okay," DeeDee said, disappointed. Potentially they'd contacted the forensic accountant for nothing. If Ptolemy had siphoned money and had the accounting books himself, he'd probably have destroyed them by now.

DeeDee declined Cordelia's invitation for afternoon tea, and went outside to find John. It seemed John had some definite, if outlandish, theories on Walter Smythe, and she wanted to hear them.

It took a long time to track him down. She went to the fountain and surrounding area first, but he wasn't there. The fountain, not unsurprisingly, had only been half cleaned, so one of the muses was still being devoured by moss, while the others had been liberated and now looked rather lovely.

She traipsed around the perimeter of the house, but again John was nowhere to be found. She passed the window of a grand drawing room, and saw Cordelia and Walter Smythe deep in conversation on an antique sofa. He was talking, and she was rapt with attention, her beautiful green eyes unblinking. Then DeeDee noticed that Walter had his hand on Cordelia's knee! She gasped and hurried away before they noticed her.

What in the heck was going on? Were they having an affair? Or was he just comforting her after the loss of "Daddy?" But it looked like more than that, it really did. She thought of the look in Cordelia's eyes, the adoring, worshipful look. She thought of Cordelia's buzzing around the kitchen, and the huge spread of food she'd laid out, and began to feel sick.

She walked away from the house into the grounds, but then realized Cecil's room had been vacated by Walter, which gave her the perfect chance to go look for the accounting books.

She hurried around to the front entrance and made her way in. Unfortunately, the only things in the drawers were neatly-folded clothes and some very faded editions of a country magazine that included articles on shooting expeditions and polo, and had classified ads for large country farms and estates. No accounting books or personal documents were to be found.

She left to pick Jake up from the car rental depot in the nearby town. They went to the hotel, took their belongings, paid up, and then went back to the manor. "The bedroom looks fine," DeeDee said. "I checked it this morning, and the fire department has given it the all-clear."

DeeDee explained her fruitless day, and Jake explained his equally fruitless trip to London. He sighed with exasperation.

"At least we may be able to wiggle some information out of this Smythe character tonight," DeeDee said. "We've been invited to a grand dinner. Like I said, their relationship is highly suspicious."

The grand dinner was held in yet another room Jake and DeeDee had never been in. It was an absolutely incredible room that looked as if it had once been a small ballroom. The ceiling was extremely high, with angels and cherubs painted on it, floating gracefully through puffy clouds and a chalky blue sky. A huge, glittering chandelier hung down over a long table that was able to easily seat twenty or more people.

The table had a fresh flower centerpiece and was laid out immaculately with polished silverware. Cordelia had requested that they wear the best clothes they'd brought along, and to meet there at 8:00 p.m.

Jake and DeeDee arrived, passable in Jake's new suit and DeeDee in a semi-formal navy dress she'd brought, to find the dining room empty. Admittedly, they were a few minutes early.

"This is so weird," DeeDee whispered to Jake. "Why is she treating this Walter Smythe guy like he's some kind of king?"

Her whisper echoed around the room, up to the heavenly roof and back again, as if all the angels were whispering derisively. Some kind of king...

"Maybe he's very rich," Jake suggested, "and she's trying to butter him up to get some manor-fixing cash."

"Not a bad theory. Or she's in love with him, and desperate to impress."

"Who's in love with whom?" Cordelia asked, making them jump as she appeared behind them with a large serving platter covered with a silver dome.

"Oh!" DeeDee said with a jolt. "In love with Ptolemy. His

girlfriend, Kelsey."

Cordelia frowned. "I thought his girlfriend was called Kelly. Anyway, Kelly, Kelsey, what's the difference?" She placed the serving platter on the table, among others that were already laid out. She smoothed her green velvet floor-length dress, which looked completely medieval, especially with her auburn hair, and looked at them with a nervous smile.

"How does everything look? Our own little medieval banquet, just as my forebears would have had, although they'd have hundreds of servants, scores of guests, and likely a number of pigs roasted on a spit for the occasion."

"It does look wonderful," Jake said, notwithstanding he couldn't see any of the food since it was all covered. It was just the polite thing to say, and, most of the time, Jake could always be counted on to say the right thing.

But DeeDee realized Cordelia's turn of phrase had given her an in. "For the occasion," she repeated, and smiled. "What are we celebrating?"

Cordelia looked down and adjusted her dress, with a private, secret smile she obviously wanted to hide, but just couldn't help. When she looked up, her eyes were gleaming with happiness. "The fact the manor hasn't been burned to smithereens, of course!"

"Ah right, yes, of course," DeeDee said, trying to keep her voice enthusiastic, while thinking it was all very strange indeed.

It soon got even stranger. Cordelia hurried to get them red wine, her red hair and velvet dress swinging out behind her as she left.

"That's a new one on me," Jake said. "Having a party because only one part of your house burned down. She seems totally manic. In all honesty, I'm a little worried about her."

"Me, too," DeeDee said. "She's been through so much lately, and the fire was a huge shock. Her whole world is changing. Maybe this is just a way for her to make herself feel better."

"I hope she calms down soon."

She was gone a rather long time, so they amused themselves by inspecting the numerous old paintings on the wall, some portraits of the Manor's former residents, some depicting country landscapes and fox hunts on horseback.

A long time after Cordelia left, Walter Smythe arrived in a tweed suit that made him a perfect caricature of a wealthy old Englishman. He had a large glass of red wine in hand.

He completely ignored DeeDee and focused on Jake. "I hear you're a celebrated investigator in Yank country! Good man!"

"Yank country?" Jake said with an amused look. "Do you mean the States? But yes, I am a private investigator. As is my wife, DeeDee, among other things."

He meant, of course, that she was also a caterer, but Walter Smythe obviously thought he meant something pejorative because he snickered and nudged Jake like it was some kind of inside joke.

"Where's your wine?" he barked at DeeDee, then turned to Jake. "Haven't you been served?"

"We were waiting for Cordelia," DeeDee said. "Have you seen her?"

"Yes. She gave me this wine when I passed by the kitchen just moments ago. She said she'd be along shortly and we should start eating without her."

"Really?" DeeDee said. "It doesn't seem right to begin without her."

He totally and completely ignored her.

120

"Come here, young man," he said to Jake jovially as he went to sit down toward the top of the table. "I want to know all about your line of business."

Jake gave DeeDee an apologetic look, and she knew what it meant. He wanted to defend her from Walter's rudeness, but he had to play along to keep him on their side. That way, Jake would be able to find out much more about him. DeeDee knew and understood that, but she couldn't deny that her pride was hurt.

She really didn't want to even listen to Walter's voice as the three of them sat down, but she had no choice. They began to eat the bread rolls that were laid out in baskets, with some fine, fresh butter that DeeDee guessed came from Killian's farm.

Walter fired question after question at Jake, but DeeDee totally tuned out, knowing listening would only serve to make her all the more annoyed, and also knowing Jake was more than capable of handling himself.

Her thoughts turned to where the accounting books could be, but that thought only frustrated her. They must be with Ptolemy.

Did Pat's sighting of Ptolemy's car have any merit? Maybe she should go into the village tomorrow and ask around. She let a picture build in her mind. Ptolemy was siphoning money, then Cecil found out. They had a blazing row, and Cecil threatened to turn Toll into the police, so Toll came back in the dead of night and killed Cecil in his sleep with a lethal injection.

But one question flashed through her head. Why would Ptolemy drive through the village? He could have driven through the country lanes, and there was far less chance of being spotted. But then if he'd met another vehicle on those narrow, winding roads, and one of them had to reverse for the other, his vehicle would have been more memorable. Perhaps he just decided to take the chance of driving through Little Dockery. It didn't exactly have a raving nightlife to speak of. She'd discovered that the pub closed at 9:00 p.m.

Hmm... well, that was a viable theory. And he also knew he'd stand a good chance of getting some money. Apparently the fortune was vast, and, as fond as she was of Ptolemy, Cordelia was bound to give him something, even if he hadn't been named in the will.

Then again, Cordelia also had the means and motive, and she certainly had been acting strangely. Of course, that could just be a side effect of the grief and stress she'd been under, or...

They were coming to the end of copious bread rolls. "Where is Cordelia?" DeeDee said.

Walter Smythe had been explaining something about quantitative easing to Jake, some financial concept or other, and paused, his hands frozen in the middle of gesticulating, and glared at her. Then he turned to Jake and continued on, as if DeeDee were a naughty child for interrupting them.

But Jake didn't ignore her. "I've been thinking the same thing. She's been gone a very long time now."

"I'm going to go look for her," DeeDee said. She actually didn't relish the prospect. It had gotten dark, and the manor was even less inviting at night than it was in the daytime. The portraits of old ancestors looked very sinister under the old lights, which flickered ominously. It was almost as if they would start talking or climb out of their frames.

Everything was cast in shadows, and the manor was so huge that anybody could be lurking in an abandoned room. In fact, DeeDee would bet a whole army could tuck themselves into nooks and crannies, ready to pounce on a passerby, and nobody would be any the wiser.

"I'll come with you," Jake said, getting to his feet.

"No, stay," Walter commanded Jake. "Call the housekeeper. She can go look for her."

DeeDee's hatred of him, and worry for Cordelia, got the better of her. "I told you earlier that there is no darn housekeeper."

Walter sniffed and looked at Jake. "Control your woman." He took the silver domes off the food and began to serve himself. "I'm certainly not going to be playing Poirot around here, and I won't sit here like a duck as you do so, either. Jake, come and sit down and eat."

Jake rolled his eyes at DeeDee. "I'm coming with you."

They left the dining room, and as soon as they closed the door, Jake burst out, "That guy!"

"I know, right?" DeeDee said, looking left and right for Cordelia as they went down the hallway. She even looked in totally silly places, like behind the curtains, but felt like she couldn't leave a stone unturned. A horrible feeling of dread was rumbling in her gut. She knew something wasn't right.

CHAPTER SIXTEEN

Unfortunately, DeeDee's terrible hunch was absolutely right.

DeeDee and Jake, becoming increasingly worried, searched the manor. They went into the kitchen. There were two wine glasses on the counter, full to the brim with red wine. But there was another one, too, and the sight of it made DeeDee's stomach drop. The third glass lay on the counter, broken. Red wine had flowed out of it onto the floor, and stained the cabinet. Its wine shimmered in the low light and looked like blood. But there was no Cordelia. The light was still on.

Jake opened the back door to the herb garden. "Cordelia?" he called out, but there was no answer.

DeeDee suggested they check Cecil's suite. Maybe all her manic enthusiasm was hiding her terrible grief, and she was missing her father. It would make sense she'd be in there, maybe to feel his presence again. But she wasn't.

The large glass-paned doors that led from the suite to the garden made DeeDee shudder in the mood she was in. The night was black, and anyone could be out there, lurking in the dark, watching Jake and DeeDee. She had horrible visions of a killer pressing their gaunt face and bloody hands up against the glass. Don't be so ridiculous, she scolded herself.

They continued their search, going first to places they knew her to frequent. Her bedroom was obviously a likely choice, but the door was locked. "Cordelia?" DeeDee said, knocking on the door. "Are you in there?" Nothing. "I understand if you don't want to come down for dinner. Could you just let us know you're all right?" But total and complete silence was the only response they got.

They were becoming frantic and started calling out her name as they rushed through the numerous dark, flickering corridors, throwing open doors to abandoned rooms, but they still couldn't find her.

They went back downstairs to the kitchen, planning to go through the herb garden and into the grounds, to see if she'd gone for one of her solitary walks to clear her head.

It was only when they got to the back door that they realized how pitch black it was out there.

"I've got my phone for a flashlight," DeeDee said, getting her smartphone from her sparkly evening clutch and turning on the flashlight feature. "Look, it's real bright."

"Ugh, I left my phone upstairs," Jake said.

"Maybe there's one in here," DeeDee said, opening the door to a small pantry where Cordelia kept various things.

DeeDee fell back onto Jake in shock and horror when she opened the door. Because there, slumped on the floor, her head flopping forward lifelessly, was Cordelia.

*****

Jake and DeeDee rode in the ambulance, looking down at Cordelia. Thankfully, Jake had found a pulse, and the ambulance was rushing to get her to the hospital to revive her. She looked horribly pale, like a corpse.

"I think we should call Toll," DeeDee said. "He's her closest family member."

"Yes," Jake agreed.

DeeDee was in shock and didn't even remember that she didn't have Ptolemy's phone number. She kept scrolling through the P section of her contacts list, wondering if she was losing her mind and actually it was a silent M or B at the beginning of his name.

But in a few moments, she snapped to her senses and said, "Maybe Cordelia has her phone on her." But even as her eyes reluctantly scanned Cordelia's frame, she knew it wasn't possible. Her medieval dress didn't have any pockets.

"Oh," Jake said. "I have Richard's business card, and it has his cell number on it. I'll call him, and he can let Ptolemy know what's happened."

Richard answered the phone immediately. DeeDee supposed with him being a senior level partner in a multinational company, he probably got calls at crazy hours on a regular basis. "Richard Boatwright-Jones."

Jake explained what had happened, and Richard surprised him by asking a thousand questions. "Which hospital? What does the ambulance staff suspect? Is her condition stable? Do they have her hooked up and properly monitored in the ambulance?"

Jake answered as best he could, referring back to the ambulance staff when needed. Richard hung up, never telling Jake whether or not he'd call Ptolemy. Jake let out a long breath and said, "Well, that was certainly a change of heart. When I met him, he sounded ambivalent about his sister. Now he's frantic."

"Maybe reality's hit home," DeeDee said sagely, "and now he knows... well, he knows he might lose her. And he's realizing how much he cares." She looked down at poor Cordelia, and wondered what in the world was going on at Dockery Manor.

As soon as the ambulance reached the hospital, Cordelia was rushed to the intensive care ward by the ER doctor and two nurses. DeeDee and Jake were allowed to hurry along behind them, but when they got to the intensive care waiting room, they could go no further.

Their adrenaline was still pumping, and they didn't feel like sitting down. Thankfully the waiting room was empty, even the front desk where the ward nurses answered questions was vacant, so they could pace about and talk freely.

"I think she's been poisoned, too," DeeDee said, fearing the worst. "I think the reason she still has a pulse is because the poison hasn't taken its full effect." She grimaced. "I'm not sure that this is going to end well."

"Maybe, but maybe not."

"But why else would she be unconscious? She didn't have any marks on her head, at least none that the first responders could see. It doesn't seem like she was knocked out."

"As far as we know, but maybe they missed something."

Jake's optimism was getting under her skin. "Wake up and smell the coffee, Jake! We were too slow. Walter got in there and tried to kill her. It just makes sense."

"I agree that it's the obvious answer," Jake said, looking at her, folding his arms, and then pursing his lips.

"And the obvious answer is usually the right one," DeeDee said. "We shouldn't have told anyone that we were investigating Cecil's murder. It was stupid. We should have thought it all out and come up with a better story. We could have said we were, I don't know, history buffs who wanted to write about Cecil's life or something. We just put all our cards on the table, actually Cordelia's cards on the table, and look at the result."

"You may be right," he said, "but we can only look forward and think positive..."

"Look forward to what?" DeeDee asked. "Cordelia's possibly dead now, and she hired us to clear her name. We not only failed at that, but we failed so spectacularly we gave the killer time to come and try to kill her.

"There's nothing else we can do now. This is a disaster. A disaster. An absolute utter and total failure. And this isn't like my catering business, where a failure means that a soufflé collapses, and you make it over again. No, in this business, people die, or the wrong people go to jail for life. No, no, no... this is too much."

DeeDee sank down on a waiting room couch, full of frustration, guilt, and worry. A million uncomfortable emotions swirled up in a muddy soup inside her head. She wished she could cry to let it all out, but tears wouldn't come.

Jake came over, sat beside her, and put his arm around her. He was silent.

After a few moments, she looked up at him. "What have we done?" she whispered.

Jake shook his head. "We don't have time to cry in our beer," he said quietly and calmly. "There are still things we have to do. For one, we need to call the police."

"Yes." DeeDee groaned and put her head in her hands. "That guy, what's his name, Officer Dean is the last person on earth I want to see right now."

"I'll try Officer Marks instead," he said. But it turned out Officer Marks wasn't in, and he got put through to Officer Dean.

Before Jake could even say anything, Officer Dean said, "I don't know what's done in America," he said disparagingly, as if everything in America must be done in an inferior way to the Great and

Marvelous Britain, "but in England, we call the police immediately at the scene of an incident." The phone was on loudspeaker. DeeDee shook her head in disgust.

"Ah," Jake said. "So you know what happened?"

"Yes." He didn't elaborate how.

DeeDee guessed the hospital must have called him. She thought quickly, and said, "To let you know Cordelia got burned?"

"Not burned," Officer Marks said haughtily. "Poisoned. I thought you were at the crime scene and in the ambulance."

"Sorry," DeeDee said. "I said burned, but I meant poisoned. I'm in a bit of shock."

"Well, you'd better get your words in order before I get up there, or you might find yourself in the slammer for the night." He slammed down the phone.

"DeeDee, you're a genius," Jake said, but his eyes didn't light up. "So she was poisoned."

CHAPTER SEVENTEEN

As DeeDee and Jake sat in the waiting room letting the horrible news that Cordelia really had been poisoned sink in, the door from the hallway opened.

Ptolemy walked in, in a mishmash ensemble of track suit pants, a knitted shirt, and pink fluffy slippers. DeeDee guessed they were probably his girlfriend's, but with Ptolemy, you couldn't be sure. Kelsey hurried in after him, a curvy, naturally pretty girl, with no makeup, and her long dark hair a slightly disheveled curtain on one side of her head. She piled it all up on top of her head and secured it with a band as Ptolemy approached them.

"What happened?" Ptolemy asked, looking ashen.

DeeDee introduced them.

"Ah!" Jake said. "I must call your father to tell him."

DeeDee touched Ptolemy on the arm. She spoke gently. "Cordelia's been poisoned, Toll." She nodded towards Ptolemy's girlfriend. "You're Kelsey, am I correct?"

She nodded, but looked at Ptolemy, clearly worried about him.

Ptolemy stared toward the doors that led to the ward. "Is she…?"

"Yes, she's in there. Maybe you can go in because you're family. I'll ring the bell and find out." She went over to the nurse's station and did so.

"So she's not..."

DeeDee knew what he meant instantly. Dead. "I don't know, Toll. I don't think so."

A thought flashed into her head out of nowhere. *If Cordelia died, wouldn't he inherit everything? It would go to Richard first, but Richard didn't want it, so surely it would be passed to Toll? She didn't know of any other relatives.*

Then another thought flashed into her mind. *What had become of Walter? Didn't he see the ambulance arrive? Why hadn't he come out of the dining room?*

Her mind was spinning in confusion. It felt like she was surrounded by monsters on every side. No one could be trusted. She felt light-headed.

A nurse came out from the double doors leading to the ward. She was about to speak, then did a double take when her eyes rested on Ptolemy. She opened her mouth to speak, but Ptolemy got there first. "Is she dead?"

"No," the nurse said. "We have her on a breathing machine. She's still unconscious, and we're running tests."

"Can I see her?" Ptolemy asked.

"No," the nurse said. "When we're finished running the tests you can. We'll come out here and get you in case of an emergency. You're welcome to wait here."

"This is an emergency!" he yelled and began swearing at her.

For a moment the nurse stared at him, then she marched right up to him, her tiny frame dwarfed by his. "If you speak to any member of the staff in that manner again, you'll be thrown out. Behave yourself." Then she marched back through the doors into the ward and out of sight.

Ptolemy began ranting, but then it seemed he lost the will to, because he stopped and flopped down in a chair.

"I think I need something to eat," DeeDee said to Jake. She was feeling a little wobbly on her feet. "I'm craving donuts." She felt she could eat about ten of them in one sitting.

"Sugar," he said. "Let's go find something." He asked Ptolemy and Kelsey if they wanted anything.

They left the ward and soon found a coffee station in one of the corridors. DeeDee ordered a hot chocolate with whipped cream, and was relieved to see donuts on display. She ordered two. She poured a ton of sugar packets into the hot chocolate, when she'd normally just have put one in, but her body was telling her that it desperately needed sugar.

Jake got a sweet tea and a huge panini filled with chicken, melted cheese, and Italian pesto.

It was hard to know where to eat. They didn't want to miss out on any news about Cordelia, so they considered going back to the waiting room. But DeeDee was bursting to talk about who, what, when, and why, and there was no way they could do that in front of Ptolemy and Kelsey. They found a table, and DeeDee told Jake about her Ptolemy-inheritance theory.

"Yes," Jake said. "Or maybe Richard is playing it cool and actually has a lot more interest in the manor, or the money, than he lets on."

"True. Or he and Ptolemy are in it together. Richard's the mastermind. Toll's the trigger man. Or in this case, the syringe man."

"He arrived extremely quickly though," Jake pointed out. "The hospital is very close to his house. It checks out that he was at home. I mean, whoever did it, unless it was Walter, would have had to have walked, likely through the back of the gardens and then the fields. It takes a long time on that route to reach anywhere you could park. I don't think he'd have had time to do all that walking, and drive back. Anyway, Kelsey will provide an alibi."

"I still think he could have done it if he hurried. And she'll just lie for him."

Jake shook his head. "Doesn't look the type to me."

"The girl hasn't said a word since she arrived."

"Gut feeling."

"What about Walter? Why didn't he come running when the ambulance came?"

"I doubt he even saw it," Jake said.

"That's a point," DeeDee said. "Since that room backs up to the garden, he probably wouldn't have heard it. They had their sirens off, and the door to the dining room was closed. Yes, that makes sense."

Jake nodded. "He's probably still eating that feast by himself, glad none of us have come back, so he doesn't have to share it."

"Hmm," DeeDee said. "I like to call him to let him know what's going on, but I know there's no phone line at the manor, so we don't have any way to contact him."

"I guess he'll just have to wonder," Jake said.

DeeDee sighed. "I just hope Cordelia pulls through."

They went back to the intensive care waiting room, gave Ptolemy and Kelsey their requested food, and sat down and waited.

Jake fell asleep in his chair. DeeDee flipped through some magazines she found on a side table, many of them a couple of years old. Right now, she was in no frame of mind to take in the fashion ideas, interior design tips, and landscape gardening information offered in the magazines.

She also couldn't think any more about who could have done this to Cordelia, and how it was connected to Cecil's murder. Her brain had totally switched off, and she couldn't get it to spark back on, no matter how hard she tried. Eventually, she, too, succumbed to sleep, the magazine sliding off her lap and onto the floor.

The next morning, she awoke with a jolt. Jake was still asleep, as was Ptolemy, still wearing Kelsey's fluffy slippers. But the owner of the slippers was missing.

DeeDee looked at her watch. It was 5:45 a.m., rather early to wake up. But once she'd opened her eyes in the mornings, she usually struggled to go back to sleep, and that was when she was in a comfy bed. Dozing back to sleep while sitting in a waiting room chair? No chance.

She was stiff from the position she'd slept in and decided a walk outside would be the best cure for that. She could stretch out and hopefully, she'd feel somewhat human again. And a strong cup of coffee would help as well.

She slipped away quietly and found Kelsey at the coffee station, ordering a flat white. "Morning, Kelsey," DeeDee said, still feeling a crick in her neck. "Sleep okay?"

Kelsey gave her a tight smile. "As well as can be expected. Would you like something?"

DeeDee ordered a cappuccino with an extra shot of espresso, to really give her some pep.

There was a sign leading to the 'Peace Garden' and DeeDee invited Kelsey to join her in the garden, hoping they could walk and talk.

It turned out the Peace Garden was just a small courtyard with a few potted plants and benches. A couple of nurses were there talking. There wasn't enough space to walk, but DeeDee gave a sigh of relief as the cold bracing air hit her skin.

They sat on a bench, sipping their coffee quite companionably. DeeDee, with her still sleepy brain, tried to come up with a way to dig for more information on Ptolemy.

But she didn't even get to open her mouth.

There was a large window from the hospital corridor onto the Peace Garden, and she got a sense somebody was watching her. When she looked, her stomach sank. It was Officer Dean, watching her.

He came outside.

"Hi, Officer Dean," DeeDee said in a friendly tone, trying to get their interaction off on the right foot. "Have you worked all through the night? That's a long shift."

"I'm working overtime," he said proudly. "I'm investigating this personally, and no one is going to get in the way. So, what do you think," he said, his eyes shining. "Cordelia busted out a syringe and injected herself to throw me off the scent? To hide the fact she killed her father."

"How can you say that?" Kelsey said, feisty as anything. "She could die."

"If she wakes up, she'll be getting a very thorough grilling from me. I'll make her wish she did die."

Kelsey, incensed, stood up. "What's your badge number? I'm reporting you to the Police Commission for inappropriate behavior."

He shrugged. "Go ahead, Miss." But from the way his eyes darted around, DeeDee knew he was secretly worried.

From that moment on, he acted in an extremely professional manner. "I would appreciate it if you two would please accompany me to the intensive care ward."

CHAPTER EIGHTEEN

Cordelia woke up, just after 7:00 a.m.

Officer Dean had already taken statements from DeeDee, Jake, Ptolemy, and Kelsey, and was on his way out, when a nurse whooped with joy. "She's awake! She's awake!" DeeDee could hear her exclaim from the corridor.

When she came into the waiting room, she was much calmer, but her eyes were shining with joy. She couldn't be too exuberant there. By then other families had arrived, and it would be insensitive to celebrate one patient's progress so loudly when others may have deteriorated, or might not make it at all.

At that very moment, as if with perfect planning, some well-wishers from Little Dockery also arrived. There was the vicar, Pat Ives and her husband, and two women DeeDee didn't know. There was no time to find out, either. Everyone wanted to see Cordelia, not make introductions.

But Officer Dean pushed himself in front of them and said, "I am going in to meet with the suspect. You people will have to wait out here."

"The suspect?" DeeDee said, outraged, at the same time as Jake, Ptolemy, and Kelsey said "the suspect?"

But he didn't have the courtesy to turn around to explain himself, and the nurse was afraid to refuse a police officer. She led him through the doors, and they all had to remain in the waiting room.

"Suspect?" Pat Ives repeated. "How can he call her such a thing, when she's just been poisoned?"

"I know!" DeeDee said. "It's so insensitive. How did you find out about it?"

"I saw the ambulance pass through the village," the vicar said. "I called the hospital to find out what was going on, but they could only confirm Cordelia was present, not what had happened to her. And they said visiting hours were over, and that I should come the next day. I called Pat to let her know, seeing as how she'd worked up at the Manor."

DeeDee's heart was beating quickly. "How did you know Cordelia had been poisoned, Pat?"

Pat brushed off the question casually. "Well, since Cecil was, I just assumed she had been, too."

DeeDee looked back at Jake, then smiled, pretending to be totally oblivious. "Would anyone like a drink while we're waiting for Cordelia? Maybe we should buy her something, too, though I'm not sure if she'll be allowed to eat anything. Pat, a coffee?"

"I'll have a cup of tea," Pat said. "That's very kind of you. What would you like, Michael?"

They asked all the members of the group, and soon had a long list of things to order. Jake and DeeDee hurried outside.

"It's her, isn't it?" DeeDee hissed. "Unless she'd spoken to Officer Dean, how could she possibly know? Like the vicar said, the hospital wouldn't give out the information. She did it, and she accidentally let that slip. She must have done it."

"I'm not sure," Jake said. "I agree that what she said sounds totally damning. But here's the question, what's the motive? She doesn't stand to gain anything from it."

"She killed Cecil because he was so unpleasant to her," DeeDee speculated. "But..." When it came to Cordelia, her mind was blank. Jake had a point. What reason would Pat have for wanting to kill Cordelia. "Maybe Cordelia was on to her and knew she'd killed Cecil?"

"But Cordelia would have told us that, wouldn't she?" Jake said. He ordered the list of drinks, then turned back to her. "Unless... she's working with someone who would gain from it."

"The only people who would gain are Ptolemy and Richard."

"Wait a minute," Jake said. The look on his face let DeeDee know his stomach had just dropped. He went eerily pale. "Oh, DeeDee, I've been so stupid."

"What? What is it?"

"The other person to gain is Walter. He said something last night, and in all the drama with Cordelia, I'd forgotten it." He looked pained. "And now we've left him in the house, alone."

"What?" DeeDee said, her pulse quickening. "Tell me what's going on!"

"He told me Cordelia didn't know anything about business affairs. And she hadn't organized any of the paperwork, but she needed to, because some things in the will weren't adding up. He said he needed to get to them, but she was resistant, and he had to get her out the way. He laughed and said maybe he'd send her to an antiques fair or something. But maybe he only said that to cover his tracks."

"Some things in the will weren't adding up," DeeDee repeated. "What's that got to do with him?"

"Exactly. I'm wondering if he's trying to work some business loophole to get his hands on Cecil's money. If not all of it, at least a large portion. He's probably in the house right now looking through papers, and doctoring them up if need be."

"I don't know," DeeDee said. "That seems like quite a leap."

"I just have a really bad feeling about it. He could change everything around and work his dark magic on Cordelia's inheritance."

"My head hurts," DeeDee said. "What I still don't understand is why Cordelia was so anxious to please him. It was like he had something she wanted."

"Maybe she knew that's why he was there," Jake said darkly. "To try to get his hands on the money."

DeeDee nodded, her brain whirring with thoughts too fast to catch up with. "So... so... He could have definitely tried to kill Cordelia. But could he have killed Cecil? Oh, and what if the person who injected Cordelia didn't mean to kill her at all, but just scare her."

"I think that might be the case," Jake said. "Or... if they meant to kill her, they wouldn't have worried about hiding their identity." His eyes widened. "She might have seen them!"

They collected the drinks and hurried back to the intensive care waiting room. Officer Dean was still inside, and everyone else waited nervously in the waiting room. DeeDee tried to veil her suspicion as she looked at Pat, then at Ptolemy. There were just too many possibilities, especially when she considered there might be a secret connection between numerous people.

As if that weren't enough, yet another person involved in it all walked in. Richard.

"Dad?" Ptolemy said, shocked.

He ignored Ptolemy and went over to the nurse behind the desk, frantic. "Where's my sister? Is she all right? Cordelia Boatwright-Jones." The situation was explained to him, and then, with a deep sigh and worried look, he walked over to Jake to shake his hand. He nodded at DeeDee and walked over to Ptolemy.

They looked at each other for a long while then Richard hugged him. Ptolemy sank into it, looking relieved, like a little boy who just wanted the affection of his father.

They all waited for a long time, desperate to see Cordelia.

Only family was let in first, so Richard and Ptolemy went in. When they came out a short while later, everyone was full of questions.

"How is she?" "Is she going to be okay?" "Can we go in and see her?"

The doctor told them she would need quite a bit of rest, but she would completely recover. When he was finished speaking to them, Richard told them that Cordelia hated hospitals, and he was paying for a private doctor and nurse to come to the manor, so that Cordelia could be attended to at home.

Jake, DeeDee, Ptolemy, Kelsey, Pat, Michael, the vicar, and the two other women, returned to Dockery Manor. Richard was staying at the hospital with Cordelia until the private doctor arrived, and would bring her back in a private ambulance.

Jake and DeeDee arrived first to find John at the entrance, putting escaped cobblestones back in their rightful places. As they made their way up the driveway, DeeDee said, "This is so confusing. Everything's going over and over in my mind, and I just can't seem to make sense of it."

"I can't say I'm making much sense of it either," Jake said. He nodded towards John. "And we've let him slip out of our thoughts, too, when he's a person who could have easily gotten in to try to kill

Cordelia."

"Yes," DeeDee said. "There just seem to be so many possibilities. So many threads to untangle."

"Let's get it straight," Jake said. "We can get a piece of paper, and write out everything we know. Who has means, who has motives, and get it all straightened out. From that we can work out what other information we need in order to figure out who did it."

"Yes, absolutely." DeeDee nodded. "But first, I want to find Walter."

They got out of their car, and let John know what had happened to Cordelia. DeeDee watched his reaction closely. He looked very shocked, and then mournful. It seemed he truly didn't know about it. Or maybe he was just a good actor...?

A person who was crazy enough to kill by sneaking around injecting people was probably treacherous enough to be a wonderful liar. But what could his motive be? DeeDee put that out of her head. They'd deal with that after they found Walter.

"Come," DeeDee said to Jake, motioning him toward the hallway that led to Cecil's room. She just had a feeling he'd be in there, and sure enough he was, sitting on the floor among a sea of papers, punching numbers into a calculator.

"Aha!" DeeDee said. Adrenaline rushed through her. She picked up a wad of paper. "Trying to work out how to get your hands on Cecil's fortune, Walter?"

The absolute fury shooting out of Walter Smythe's eyes made him look like a demon. "Yes, yes, I am. And if you so much as breathe a word about it to Cordelia, I'd be very happy to make whatever sort of arrangements it would take to get you two out of the way."

"Oh, we know that," Jake said. "We know exactly what you're capable of. You proved that last night, when you poisoned Cordelia."

Walter Smythe's eyes popped open in surprise. "When I what? What on earth are you talking about?"

Jake and DeeDee looked at each other, surprise and disbelief showing on their faces.

DeeDee continued on, but her confidence wavered, and her voice along with it. "You can act as surprised as you want," she said. "We know you came here and killed Cecil Boatwright-Jones. Then, when you didn't receive any money, you came down here to work out how you could get it. And when Cordelia wouldn't let you go snooping, you poisoned her to get her out of your way."

"Preposterous!" he said. "Everything you've just said is a complete load of claptrap. I didn't kill anybody, or try to kill anybody. I wouldn't know how to poison someone, and it's not in my nature. I assumed Cordelia had retired to her bedroom last night because the company was overwhelming, what with her being such a hermit, I've known it to happen."

"She was in the hospital, nearly dying," DeeDee said. "In the intensive care ward."

"Well, thank you very much for keeping me in the loop," he said sarcastically. "Now, if you don't mind, I am trying to clear up some of Cecil's unresolved business matters. Yes, some money may be on its way to me as a result, but that is no crime. I would appreciate if you butted out."

Jake and DeeDee, having run out of things to say, left the room. Once they'd closed the door, DeeDee hit herself on the head. "You see? I'm not in the zone. I shouldn't have accused him. It could well be him, but now he knows we're onto him and he'll hide evidence."

"We're all over the place," Jake agreed.

"Let's do our list right now. Coffee?"

"Absolutely."

They went into the kitchen, and DeeDee felt deeply uncomfortable. The wine glasses were in exactly the same place as they had been the previous night when they'd found Cordelia slumped on the floor. The wine had dried up on the cabinet where it had dripped down, and looked even more like blood.

DeeDee sighed. "I'd like to clean it up, but I'd better not, or Officer Dean will accuse me of tampering with evidence if I do."

"You're right," Jake said. "That's the last thing we'd need right now."

DeeDee set about making the coffee, while Jake rummaged in the drawers, and found a pad of paper and a pen.

Soon they were sitting in the grand drawing room, where Cordelia had laid out such a spread for Walter the previous day. It felt like a lifetime ago. They sipped their coffee, and began to analyze the suspects.

CHAPTER NINETEEN

"Okay," Jake said, writing while he talked. "People who could have done it... Pat Ives, the caregiver, John Bowen, the handyman, Walter Smythe, the..."

"The absolute and complete... Well, I won't finish that sentence before I curse," DeeDee said. "Ptolemy Boatwright-Jones, the grandson. Richard Boatwright-Jones, the son. Oh, and the possibility that Cordelia could have killed her father, and then someone else poisoned her."

"Possibly, though it seems unlikely they'd use the same method," Jake said.

"Maybe it wasn't the same," DeeDee said. "After all, Cecil's injection was successful. Cordelia's wasn't."

"True. We can rule out the idea that Cordelia did it herself to throw everyone off the scent that she killed Cecil, because she wouldn't have been able to drag herself into the pantry," Jake said.

"Yes. Unless she had an accomplice."

"Ptolemy, because they both wanted to inherit. She killed Cecil, then he came here and injected her with a non-lethal dose, to make it look like there was a killer on the loose, and clear Cordelia's name,"

Jake said.

"That would make sense," DeeDee said. "Actually, that would make a lot of sense."

"I suppose Richard could also be in on it."

"Although he seems to have enough money on his own."

"Seems being the operative word," Jake said. "There are lots of people who earn huge amounts of money, but are still in debt. Overspending, bad investments, the list goes on and on."

"That's true," DeeDee said as she took a sip of coffee. Her brain finally felt less clouded. "With the family members, it's much easier to ascertain a motive, because of the inheritance. We also have a very clear motive for Walter Smythe. Money, again."

She sighed just at the thought of him. He exhausted her. "But what about Pat Ives and John Bowen? They would both have had the means. They know the village very well, and I'm sure they could have navigated walking through those fields to come and do the dirty work. But why?"

"Hmm..." Jake said. "Well, we know both of them were ill-treated by Cecil. Of course, being his caregiver, Pat got more of the brunt of his anger. But then John seems very sensitive, so even the occasional insult from Cecil could have been enough to send him over the edge."

"Yes," DeeDee said. "And perhaps he didn't like begging for money from Cecil."

"It's likely."

"But... do you really think if John had done it, he'd have used poison?" DeeDee mused. "For one thing, would he have had enough money to keep buying the drug over and over like Officer Marks said the killer would have done? And the syringe?"

"Maybe he's a drug user."

DeeDee shrugged. She hadn't thought of that. "Could be. But... as they say, 'poison is a woman's weapon.'"

"Hmm. You could be right. If I picture him murdering Cecil, I'd think it would be more like hitting him over the head with a blunt object."

"Yes, I agree," DeeDee said. "And why would he hurt Cordelia? They seem to dote on each other."

"True. Although that could be an act on his part," Jake said. "Maybe he thought if he got them both out of the way, he could have the mansion to himself? Wait, no, he knew about Ptolemy, so that wouldn't make sense."

"No, I don't think so. But again, with Pat Ives, I'm coming up with a blank when it comes to motive. I could see her using poison, especially as a healthcare provider. But why? Okay, so maybe she kills Cecil for being rude to her, but that seems kind of farfetched. And then, why try to kill Cordelia? And, being a healthcare provider, she wouldn't be likely to get the dosage wrong, would she?"

"Good point," Jake said. "She'd have gotten it correct. But why kill Cordelia anyway, like you said? I don't think she'd stand to benefit in any way."

"Right," DeeDee said as she looked over their list. "Walter, Ptolemy, and Richard seem to be our most likely suspects. We need to find out where Walter was on the night Cecil died. I don't know how, but maybe we can make it work."

"Good point," Jake said, noting it down.

"And where was Ptolemy last night? Can Kelsey verify he was at home with her? I'll tackle that. We also need to find out where Richard was. Because if they were working together, Richard could have been the one who was here last night. Maybe he pretended to be up in London. I wonder if it's possible to trace his location from the phone call you made to him?"

"I'll bet the police could do it," Jake said. "But I don't think Officer Dean will be jumping at the chance to do us any favors."

"Agreed," DeeDee said. "I think we need to dig a little more into Richard breaking all contact with Cecil, however long ago it was. Obviously, we can talk to Cordelia about that, but maybe we should do some independent research on that, too. See what we can find out in the village?"

"Good plan," Jake said. "We've got a lot to do."

"Yes," DeeDee agreed. "And I wonder what we'll do for lunch, too. I might whip something up."

"Sure, if you'd like," Jake said. "Or we could get something from the pub, if you don't think you'll have the time."

"You're right," DeeDee said. "We need to investigate, and pronto, before someone else falls down with a needle stuck in their neck. Who knows? Maybe that's why Richard decided to bring her back from the hospital? To finish off the job he botched."

Jake visibly shuddered. "I hadn't thought of that. We'd better keep a close eye on him."

"Yes. I can't wait to speak to Cordelia," DeeDee said. "For now, I'm going to try and see what I can find out from Kelsey."

"I'm going to dig out whatever dirt I can on both Walter Smythe and Richard Boatwright-Jones. Like where Walter was on the night Cecil died, and where Richard was, as well as some background information on the pair of them. I'll do a mix of online research and then I'll go into the village."

"Sounds like a plan," DeeDee said. "And if the people who have gathered here at the manor want food from the pub in town, I'll give you a call, so you can order some."

"Let's do it," he replied.

They gave each other a high five and Jake left to drive into the village.

DeeDee made her way to the kitchen, which she found had filled up with people sitting around the large kitchen table.

"Oh, no," she said, walking in and seeing that the wine had been cleaned up and the two unbroken glasses washed. "That could have been part of the evidence."

"Oh dear," the vicar said. She was standing at the side, making tea and coffee for everyone, while Pat bustled around mixing ingredients for what appeared to be a cake. "I didn't even think of that."

DeeDee sighed. "Never mind. I just don't think Officer Dean will be very happy. I expect he'll be coming over here at some point."

"Yes," Pat said. "I should hope so! He hasn't been very effective in investigating what happened to Cecil, and now the evil person has struck again. Who knows who might be the next victim? Are they trying to take out the whole Boatwright-Jones family?"

"Don't say that," Kelsey said, putting her arm around Ptolemy protectively.

"She could be right," Ptolemy said darkly. "Who knows at this point?"

"Are you making a cake?" DeeDee asked Pat.

"Yes," Pat said proudly. "A Victoria sponge cake. I think we could all do with having our spirits lifted."

"You're right," DeeDee said. "My husband has gone into the village, and I wondered whether we should make an order for him to get something from Little Dockery Arms."

"I was going to pop back home to pick up some things to make a shepherd's pie," Pat said.

"Oh, don't trouble yourself," said one of the women DeeDee didn't know. "There are so many of us it would be much easier to just get it from the pub."

Pat looked extremely annoyed - her desire to always be the hostess cropping up again - but fixed her face into a smile. "Well, if you insist. Anyway, lunch is still quite a while off. We'll have the cake this morning and then we can see what we'd like for lunch."

"I agree," DeeDee said. She was thinking about how she was going to get Kelsey away from everyone so she could talk to her. Then an idea popped into her mind. "Kelsey, why don't you come with me for a moment? I want to make sure Cordelia's room is in order when she arrives from the hospital."

Kelsey looked a little confused, as in, why me, but she went along with DeeDee.

They went upstairs, and DeeDee used the opportunity to ask her if Ptolemy had been home the previous night. "I'm going to be honest with you," DeeDee said. "I just want to eliminate him as a possible suspect."

"He was home," Kelsey said. "And I'm not just saying that because I'm his girlfriend. He really was, I promise. And to prove I'm telling you the truth, I'll tell you this, he was out on the night his grandfather was killed. But I know he didn't do it, since he was with one of his friends."

"Okay," DeeDee said, not sure whether she should believe Kelsey or not.

They fixed up Cordelia's room, which was already pretty clean. All they had to do was change the bedsheets and clear the bedside tables of clutter.

When they'd finished, they went back downstairs to the kitchen. The Victoria sponge cake was in the oven, and the scent of that, mixed with coffee and tea, made for a comforting, homely atmosphere. Pat had called John in, and he stood in the doorway to the herb garden, sipping his tea, looking uncomfortable among the other people.

One down, DeeDee thought. *I know where Ptolemy was last night, or at least I have a promise of where he was. Now for Richard.*

But Richard, Cordelia, and her private doctor hadn't arrived yet. She took out her phone, while she was nursing a cup of sweet tea Pat had given her, and began to do her own little investigation.

She accessed the internet on her cell phone and typed in the name, Richard Boatwright-Jones. She didn't find anything particularly interesting. It was mainly about his career, such as interviews he'd given about the tax implications of new legislation being proposed by the government.

He'd written a very dry blog post for his company, which also came up in the search results, but there was nothing about his personal life. Although he was well-known in his own field, he wasn't famous enough to have a personal bio about him on sites such as Wikipedia. She really didn't find anything of interest.

Next DeeDee tried Richard Boatwright-Jones Little Dockery. But there was nothing there of note. She sighed deeply, then decided to try, Little Dockery 1990. It was about thirty years ago in the timeframe she'd been given when Richard might have stopped all contact with his father.

There was nothing, nothing, nothing for a long time. There was another Little Dockery, in Ireland, so she kept getting results mixed in from that. Finally, she tried, Little Dockery Cotswolds 1990.

That led her into an archive of articles from the Gloucester Herald from the 1990s. She couldn't find any mention of Little Dockery, but was drawn in by how fascinating the stories were in the 1990s. Salman Rushdie's fatwa renewed. Stories about Princess Diana and Prince Charles visiting Budapest. DeeDee had always liked her. IRA car bombs detonated. Margaret Thatcher resigning as Prime Minister.

And then she clicked on an article that made her blood run cold, because of its content. Even worse, there was a picture of the young face that accompanied the story. Blood rushed to her brain. She wanted to stand up, but she was afraid to because she felt so dizzy. She took a couple of deep breaths, then put a smile on her face, and casually left the room. "I'm going to the ladies room," she said to the people assembled in the kitchen.

As soon as she was out of the room, she rushed through the corridor, out of the front door, and down the pathway, making sure she was well out of earshot of anyone before she called Jake. Her fingers shook as she pressed in his phone number.

CHAPTER TWENTY

After DeeDee called Jake and told him about the article she'd found, she sent a copy of it to Jake. He said he'd get back to the manor as soon as he could, but there was something he had to do first. The meals from Little Dockery Arms were forgotten. DeeDee hovered near the front of the manor, biting her nails, which was quite uncharacteristic of her, as she anxiously waited for Jake to return.

Richard, Cordelia, and the new doctor arrived in the private ambulance before Jake did. Cordelia was taken out of the ambulance and put in a wheelchair. It was the first time DeeDee had seen her awake and conscious since the night before. She had an IV drip and some wires hooked up to her, but otherwise she looked surprisingly healthy.

"DeeDee!" Cordelia said. "Thank you so very much for taking care of me last night. The hospital staff told me what happened."

"Don't thank me for that," DeeDee said. "I'm just glad you're okay."

Cordelia smiled. "This old girl's on the mend. Don't you worry. Everything's going to be fine." She said it emphatically, even aggressively. Her eyes looked desperate when she asked. "How's the investigation going?"

DeeDee moved closer to her. "I'm really sorry," she said, keeping her voice down. "I'm sorry we didn't finish up in time, before someone hurt you."

"Nonsense."

"May I just ask you something really quickly?" DeeDee said. She lowered her voice to a whisper, not wanting anyone else to hear what she said.

"Of course."

"I couldn't help noticing that you were trying to get on Walter's good side. Why was that?"

Cordelia looked pained. "I hope you won't think less of me, DeeDee."

"I won't, I promise."

"He's a very wealthy man," Cordelia said. "I thought if I treated him well, he might contribute toward the manor renovations."

"Okay, I understand," DeeDee said with a nod. She thought quickly. "I'm assuming you didn't see who injected you last night?"

"No. I was standing there pouring wine, and the next thing I knew, I woke up in the hospital feeling like I'd drunk every bottle of wine in the house, plus the contents of a well-stocked wine cellar."

DeeDee nodded. "I thought as much."

But it turned out DeeDee didn't need Cordelia's eyewitness account, because Jake had found something better. Much better. And in combination with DeeDee's evidence, it was damning.

For once, DeeDee was hoping that Officer Dean would show up, but he didn't.

Richard wheeled Cordelia into the house, and they all went into the kitchen to eat cake and have tea, and for Cordelia to be flooded with well wishes and affection.

DeeDee was the only one who was nervous, and every moment in the kitchen stretched out to what seemed to be an absolute eternity to her.

But soon, everyone was gathered in the kitchen, Walter Smythe included. He'd sniffed the scent of the cake, and he'd come to the kitchen to have some. Pat had absolutely insisted he stay, and somehow, she managed to charm him.

Finally, DeeDee heard the sound of Jake pulling up in the car. She went out to meet him.

"Do you have it?" she asked.

"Yes," he said. "I've called Officer Dean, and hopefully he'll be here soon."

DeeDee breathed in and out. "Are we sure we're right? We're not wrong and getting carried away, are we?"

"No," Jake said. "I don't think so. When you sent me that article it made my blood run cold."

"Mine, too." She took another deep breath. "Shall we go in and do this then? Everyone's gathered in the kitchen having cake."

"Let's get it over with," he said, looking pale.

They walked in, and Pat started fussing around Jake immediately, offering him tea and cake.

"No, thank you," he said loudly. "I don't accept refreshments from murderers."

Pat jerked back like he'd slapped her in the face. "What?" she said, then laughed.

Everyone else gasped.

"Do you mean...?" Cordelia said, suddenly looking haggard and distraught.

"Yes," DeeDee said. "Look at this." She went around the room, showing everyone the picture from the article. "This is many years ago, but that's Pat's face, isn't it?"

"I will simply not have this!" Pat's husband Michael said angrily. "Stop this, now!"

But Jake and DeeDee ignored him. "Her name wasn't always Pat Ives," DeeDee said. "It used to be Carol Jamieson. And she was tried before a judge and jury for poisoning young children in her care, children with special needs."

A ripple of shock went through the room.

"No," Cordelia said, looking at Pat with her mouth open.

"*An investigation was started at Gloucester Royal Hospital when there was a higher than usual fatality rate at the Hazelnut Ward,*" DeeDee read. She scanned the rest and said, "There wasn't enough evidence to convict her for the murders, but there was a case where she injected a child who didn't die, and there was enough evidence for that. She was sentenced to four years in prison, it says here. When she got out of prison, she changed her name and moved here."

Pat laughed. "Have you told quite enough silly fairytales yet?" She cut herself another piece of Victoria sponge cake and bit into it aggressively.

"Let me ask you this," Jake said. "The old people she so kindly looked after in the village. Did any of them die?"

Cordelia gasped. "Some did. Pat said it was old age."

156

"This is ridiculous," Michael said. "Stop it! Stop it now, I tell you!" He grabbed Jake by the shoulders and shook him.

Jake pushed him back, and he stumbled against the counter. Pat caught him and made a big fuss over him. "I'll have you arrested for assault!" she said to Jake, pointing her finger in his face.

"No," Jake said very calmly. "You'll be arrested for murder."

"That wasn't me," Pat said. "And even if it were, how could you prove I committed this murder? You've no proof."

Richard nodded gravely. "Jake, DeeDee, I have no doubt that you're right about this murderous scum. But she has a point. What ties her to the murder?"

DeeDee couldn't help but smile. She drew two wads of toilet paper from Jake's bag, and took them over to the kitchen table. Then she carefully unwrapped them, taking care not to touch them and get her fingerprints on them.

"Is this good enough?" she asked. In one wad of toilet paper was a box of potassium chloride. In the other, was a syringe. "The door to your home was open, as usual in the village, so Jake went in and found these in one of your drawers."

"I told you it was her," Ptolemy said loudly. "I told you," he repeated to Kelsey.

"And to me," DeeDee said. "You said she freaked you out, big time. Looks like your instincts were right about her."

Michael turned to Pat, shocked. "This can't be true, can it? Can it?"

Pat's chest was rising up and down with frantic breaths. She looked all around the room, at each and every one of them, and probably saw it was useless to pretend anymore. "Yes, I did it, she blurted out."

Michael clamped his hand over his mouth and stared at her for a long time, tears welling up in his eyes. Finally, he found his voice and said, "But why?"

"Unfortunately, Carol Jamieson is one of the worst kind of murderers there is," DeeDee said.

"She's a serial murderer who kills for nothing other than the thrill of it," Jake said. "She's a total and complete psychopath."

All of a sudden, Pat began to wail loudly. "I'm sorry, I'm sorry. Cecil told me to kill him! It was euthanasia. And I didn't kill you, Cordelia, did I? I didn't even want to kill you, I just wanted to come and be your caregiver. Is that so wrong?"

Everybody agreed it was the most wrong thing they'd ever heard of in their entire lives.

As did Officer Dean.

As did the jury gathered to judge her.

As did the judge, who sentenced her to thirty-five years in prison.

EPILOGUE

A few months later it was the start of the Christmas season. A cold wind was blowing across Puget Sound, but DeeDee and Jake were enjoying a cozy night in with their two dogs, Balto and Yukon. They were enjoying sipping on hot spiced cider, and making plans for when DeeDee's grown kids would join them for the holidays.

DeeDee's favorite Christmas candle was burning, the perfect holiday scents of cinnamon, apple, ginger, and their fir tree, filled their home with wonderful smells. All felt right with the world.

The Christmas tree was twinkling with its warm white lights and the dappled light of the moon rippled on the Sound outside. The warm, cheerful sounds of a Christmas comedy movie was playing on the TV in the background. DeeDee was in the process of cooking a comforting meal consisting of a red wine beef stew with potatoes au gratin, followed by a cinnamon-apple pie, while Jake was busy stringing up more Christmas decorations.

They'd taken a long break from investigating any serious cases since they'd returned from England. DeeDee had placed her primary focus on her catering business, and it was doing very well.

Jake and Al had been doing more due diligence work for investors, since that type of case involved far less danger to them, which kept Cassie happy. DeeDee and Jake were still a little rattled by finding a psychopath serial killer. Especially one who had hurt children in the past. They needed a little time to regroup and get back to their normal life.

Once all the food prep was done, DeeDee sat on one of the stools at the kitchen island, and checked her phone.

"I got an email from Ptolemy," she said to Jake.

"Really? What does he have to say?"

"*Hi DeeDee and Jake. My auntie and my dad say hi and thank you for all you did for us. They also wanted you to see this video.* Jake, come look at it with me."

She pressed play on the video.

It started from a location by the fountain, which was now gleaming with water spilling from the jars of the muses. Then the camera turned the corner and zoomed in on the mansion.

"Oh my goodness," DeeDee said. "It looks fantastic! What incredible restoration."

"It is," Jake said. "You wouldn't even know that the West Wing had burned."

"No, you wouldn't."

The driveway was pristine. Cordelia's old red rust bucket of a car that looked like it would fall apart at any moment was no longer there. There were a few cars in the driveway, but DeeDee instinctively knew that the small little green hatchback, which was new and shiny, was Cordelia's. For the first time, they could even see the old Roman bridge in the distance.

Then the camera went inside the manor, and the sight took DeeDee's breath away. There was an enormous Christmas tree in the middle of the hallway, and all the antiques had been polished and were shining brightly. The wall tapestries were likewise bright and clean. The stained-glass window in the back let in rays of perfect, crisp light.

It made DeeDee smile.

But what made DeeDee smile more was all the people who were there.

Cordelia was buzzing around like a honey bee, putting finishing touches on everything. She looked absolutely radiant with her auburn hair tied up in a chic chignon and a deep red velvet dress flowing around her.

"We're opening to the public today!" Ptolemy said from behind the camera.

He panned over to Richard, who was looking at everything and smiling. "It certainly looks like he's had a change of heart," Jake said. "Since Cordelia was hurt, he's realized he does care about his family, and he wants to be a part of the manor's future."

"Yes," DeeDee said. She just couldn't stop smiling.

Kelsey was there too, looking healthy and happy. DeeDee scanned her left hand, but there was no ring. *Not ready yet, eh, Toll?* she thought as she laughed out loud.

But what DeeDee loved to see the most was what she saw just before the video ended. John, who looked much more washed and tamed than he previously had, leaned in and gave Cordelia a kiss on the cheek! DeeDee replayed the video, just that part, to make sure she had it right. She did!

"Well," DeeDee said, her cheeks flushing pink. "She wanted to clear her name to get her inheritance to restore the manor house and make her ancestors happy. I'd say mission accomplished."

Jake took his spiced cider and toasted it with her. "Amen to that," he said, giving her a quick kiss on the lips. "Amen to that."

RECIPES

VICTORIA SPONGE CAKE

Ingredients:
12 tbsp. unsalted butter, softened, more for greasing pans
1 ⅓ cups all-purpose flour
3 ¼ tsp. baking powder
½ tsp. kosher salt
¾ cup plus 2 tbsp. granulated sugar
3 large eggs, room temperature
2 tbsp. milk
½ cup raspberry jam, or more if preferred
1 cup heavy cream
1 tbsp. confectioners' sugar, more for dusting
¼ tsp. vanilla extract

Directions:
Preheat oven to 350 degrees and place a rack in the center of oven. Grease and line the bottoms of two 8-inch round cake pans with butter and parchment paper.

In a medium bowl, whisk together flour, baking powder, and salt. In another bowl beat butter and sugar until light and fluffy, about 3 minutes. Beat in eggs, one at a time, then beat in milk, scraping down sides of the bowl as necessary. Mix in flour mixture until combined, then scrape into prepared cake pans, smoothing the top.

Bake cakes until golden brown and a toothpick inserted in the center comes out clean, about 25 - 30 minutes. Let cool for 10 minutes, then unmold them onto a wire rack to cool completely, flat side down.

Transfer one cake to a serving platter, and spread jam evenly on top. Put heavy cream, confectioner's sugar and vanilla into a bowl and beat until it holds stiff peaks. Spoon about half the whipped cream on top of jam, then top with remaining cake. Dust with confectioners' sugar and serve immediately with the extra whipped cream on the side.

TOAD IN THE HOLE

Ingredients:
1 lb. fresh sausage links (Whatever you prefer. Classically, it would be English sausages, or bangers.)
2 tbsp. canola oil
1 cup milk
1 cup all-purpose flour
3 large eggs
Pinch of salt

Directions:
Preheat the oven to 425 degrees.

Place the sausages in a 9" x 13" baking dish. Drizzle oil on them and bake for about 15 minutes.

Meanwhile, whisk together milk, flour, eggs, and salt. Mixture should have the consistency of heavy cream. Pour into the pan around the sausages, and return to the oven. Bake for 20 minutes, or until the batter is puffed and deep golden. Serves 4 - 6. Enjoy!

CHICKEN, CHEESE AND PESTO PANINI

Ingredients:
4 boneless skinless chicken breasts
3 tbsp. olive oil
1 tbsp. fresh minced garlic
1 tbsp. dried Italian seasoning
Salt and pepper to taste
4 slices provolone cheese (Feel free to substitute another cheese,)
¾ cup pesto sauce (bottled or homemade)
8 slices Italian bread or ciabatta rolls
2 tbsp. olive oil, for brushing on bread

Directions:
Pound the chicken fillets between two pieces of plastic wrap until thin. Marinate in oil, garlic, pepper, and Italian seasoning for about 1 ½ hours.

Add olive oil to a frying or sauté pan. Season the breasts with salt and pepper. Cook the chicken over medium heat for about 5 minutes per side, or until golden brown and cooked through.

Remove from pan. Top each chicken piece with a slice of cheese. Spread one side of each bread slice with pesto sauce. Place the chicken on one piece of pesto-smeared bread and top with another piece of pesto bread to form a sandwich. Brush the outside of the bread with olive oil.

Heat a grill pan or a 10-inch skillet on medium high heat. Place the panini in the pan (two at a time).

Weigh the panini down with another heavy skillet and top with a heavy can (a very large can of tomato juice works great for this). Cook for about 3 minutes, or until bread is toasted. (I use bricks covered with tin foil as weights.)

Turn the panini, and weigh it down again. Toast for another 3 minutes. Remove from pan and cut in half. Serve and enjoy!

FRIED (FRY) BREAD

Ingredients:
1 cup all-purpose flour
1 ½ tsp. baking powder
¼ tsp. salt
½ cup milk
Vegetable oil (Enough to reach 1" depth.)
Honey or syrup for dipping

Directions:
In a deep cast iron skillet or heavy saucepan heat about 1 inch of oil to 350 degrees. If you don't have a deep-fry thermometer to attach to the pan, drop a little water in the oil. Oil is ready when the water sizzles on contact.

Combine the flour, baking powder, and salt in a bowl. Mix well to blend. Add the milk and stir until the dough holds together. Knead 3 or 4 times on a floured surface.

Divide the dough into four uniform pieces and shape each into a ball. Roll each ball of dough into a circle to desired thickness with a lightly floured rolling pin. Make a depression in the center of each round of dough.

Carefully slide one or two of the flattened dough balls into the hot oil and fry for about 1 to 2 minutes on each side, or until lightly browned.

Remove the fried dough to paper towels to drain. Serve with honey or syrup and enjoy!

SCONES

Ingredients:
2 cups all-purpose flour, plus more for hands and work surface
½ cup granulated sugar

½ tsp. salt
2 ½ tsp. baking powder
½ cup unsalted butter, frozen
½ cup heavy cream (plus 2 tbsp. for brushing)
1 large egg
1 ½ teaspoons pure vanilla extract
1 - 1 ½ cups additions such as chocolate chips, berries, nuts etc.

Optional: ½ - 1 tsp. ground cinnamon and/or coarse sugar. Toppings such as vanilla frosting, salted caramel, lemon frosting, maple frosting, brown butter frosting, lemon curd, orange frosting, raspberry frosting, dusting of confectioners' sugar. Your choice.

Directions:

Whisk flour, sugar, salt, and baking powder together in a large bowl. Grate the frozen butter using the large openings on a box grater. Add butter to the flour mixture and combine with a pastry cutter, two forks, or your fingers until the mixture comes together in pea-sized crumbs. Put mixture in the refrigerator or freezer while you mix the wet ingredients together.

Whisk ½ cup heavy cream, egg, and vanilla together in a small bowl. Remove the flour mixture from the freezer and drizzle the cream mixture over it. Add in the additions, then mix together until everything appears moistened.

To make triangle scones: Pour the mixture onto a floured board. With floured hands, work dough into a ball. If you feel it's too sticky, add a little more flour. If it seems too dry, add 1 - 2 tbsp. heavy cream. Press into an 8-inch disc. With a sharp knife, cut into 8 wedges. For smaller scones, press dough into two 5-inch discs and cut each into 8 wedges.

Brush scones with remaining heavy cream and for extra crunch, sprinkle with coarse sugar. Place scones on a plate or parchment lined baking sheet and refrigerate for at least 15 minutes.

Preheat oven to 400 degrees. After refrigerating, arrange scones 2

- 3 inches apart on the prepared baking sheet(s).

Bake for 18 - 26 minutes or until golden brown around the edges and lightly browned on top. Larger scones take closer to 25 minutes. Remove from the oven and cool for a few minutes before topping with the optional toppings listed in the ingredients. Serve and enjoy!

LEAVE A REVIEW

I'd really appreciate it you could take a few seconds and leave a review of Murder at the Manor.

Just go to the link below. Thank you so much, it means a lot to me ~ Dianne

http://getbook.at/MANOR

Paperbacks & Ebooks for FREE

Go to www.dianneharman.com/freepaperback.html and get your FREE copies of Dianne's books and favorite recipes immediately by signing up for her newsletter.

Once you've signed up for her newsletter you're eligible to win three paperbacks. One lucky winner is picked every week. Hurry before the offer ends!

ABOUT THE AUTHOR

Dianne lives in Huntington Beach, California, with her husband, Tom, a former California State Senator, and her boxer dog, Kelly. Her passions are cooking, reading, and dogs, so whenever she has a little free time, you can either find her in the kitchen, playing with Kelly in the back yard, or curled up with the latest book she's reading. Her award-winning books include:

Cedar Bay Cozy Mystery Series

Cedar Bay Cozy Mystery Series - Boxed Set

Liz Lucas Cozy Mystery Series

Liz Lucas Cozy Mystery Series - Boxed Set

High Desert Cozy Mystery Series

High Desert Cozy Mystery Series - Boxed Set

Northwest Cozy Mystery Series

Northwest Cozy Mystery Series - Boxed Set

Midwest Cozy Mystery Series

Midwest Cozy Mystery Series - Boxed Set

Jack Trout Cozy Mystery Series

Cottonwood Springs Cozy Mystery Series

Cottonwood Springs Mystery Series – Boxed Set

Midlife Journey Series

Midlife Journey Series – Boxed Set

The Holly Lewis Mystery Series

The Holly Lewis Mystery Series – Boxed Set

Red Zero Series

Black Dot Series

Coyote Series

Newsletter
If you would like to be notified of her latest releases please go to www.dianneharman.com and sign up for her newsletter.

Website: www.dianneharman.com,
Blog: www.dianneharman.com/blog
Email: dianne@dianneharman.com

PUBLISHING 2/6/20

HOLLY AND THE RUINED PARTY

BOOK 6

HOLLY LEWIS MYSTERY SERIES

http://getbook.at/HRP

Nancy Drew fans, here's a book just for you!

A surprise party at a church

To celebrate her aunt Fiona's success as a fashion designer

Streamers, banners, and food

All destroyed on the day of the party

Who did it and why?

When the party Holly has carefully planned is maliciously destroyed hours before it's to take place, her friends and family frantically work to salvage it.

But who would want to ruin a party? Doesn't everyone love a party? Was it someone who had a grudge against Fiona? Or maybe against Holly?

Holly and Wade are afraid if they don't find the person responsible, they'll do something even more damaging during the party, like harming someone at the party.

This is the sixth book in the popular Holly Lewis Mystery Series by two-time USA Today Bestselling Author, Dianne Harman.

Open your smartphone, point and shoot at the QR code below. You will be taken to Amazon where you can pre-order 'Holly and The Ruined Party'.

(Download the QR code app onto your smartphone from the iTunes or Google Play store in order to read the QR code below.)

Made in United States
Troutdale, OR
07/16/2023

11285517R00108